Mia Pride

For Matt, my real-life hero.

Thank you for loving me and my kids unconditionally and for showing me that there are truly good men in this world.

Chapter 1

Cornwall, England

1556

"Curse it all, Ruby!" Papa slammed his fist on the intricately carved wooden banister for what felt like the hundredth time that night, the vein in his neck throbbing as it did when she defied him, which seemed to be more and more as of late. "William and the other guests will be here shortly and I expect you to welcome him the way a future wife should!"

Controlling the desire to roll her eyes and stomp her foot, Ruby put her hands on her hips and stared her papa in his bloodshot brown eyes. He truly had not been sleeping well and she wondered if it was her doing. Yet, this was her life and one could not raise a strong-willed woman bred from gentle pirates, then expect her to fall into line as requested. "You are marrying me to that boorish man to intentionally stifle my spirit! To keep me out of the family business. I am not a silly little woman, Papa. I know why you are marrying me off to the Vice-Admiral of the Royal Navy. And if you think he does not know that we are all pirates, then—"

"Privateers. Smugglers, even. Not pirates," her father chided with pride and she withheld a rude snort. The Berry family had always been, and would always be, pirates. Her father, Thomas Berry, was well known as a gentleman pirate, even to the queen who allowed such things as long as the plunder always came from the enemy and was acquired outside of English waters.

"Papa, you are a gentleman through and through, as all know. But, you are a gentleman who has barrels of whiskey, coins, and other contraband in our manor's cellar. You named me after your favorite gemstone, one that you acquired from a Spanish ship your men once plundered! Call it what you want, but it does not change who we are and what my legacy is. I wish to help. I do not want to be married to a man twice my age who will expect me to sit quietly in fine gowns, embroidering while I am surrounded by servants and screaming children as I grow wide and docile. That is not who I am."

"Which is precisely why you will marry William, Ruby Clair Berry. I will not have you living a dangerous existence. Do not forget what happened to your cousin…"

Now, Ruby did sigh loudly, feeling both aggravated and aggrieved. Every time someone brought up her poor, idiotic cousin Maude, it sent chills up her spine. But, she was not Maude, who had no adventure in her bones, nor common sense in her head. "What happened to Maude aboard that ship is most unfortunate. But, I shall not trip on my own skirts and fall overboard while at sea."

"Perhaps not, but you can come across any number of dangers that are not of your doing."

A loud knock came from the front door and Ruby froze, closing her eyes and biting her lip. Her betrothed was here. He was not unattractive. A man of forty years, he had begun to gray at the temples but he otherwise seemed in good health and had a fair disposition. But, he was droll. As droll as attempting to watch leaves blow in the wind on a still afternoon. And there was no way he would ever keep Ruby out of trouble.

"He is here," her father whispered and leaned forward, shoving his finger in her face. "I expect you to behave like the lady you are, Ruby." Papa walked away and stood with his hands behind his back, straightening his face, as if he had not just been shouting at his daughter.

"Here we go," Ruby muttered under her breath, flinging a ringlet of golden hair over her shoulder and smoothing out her new royal-blue damask gown that her mother had made just for this dinner.

"Oh! The Vice-Admiral has arrived!" her mother, Penelope, tittered as she zoomed into the room like a canary with a broken wing, spinning in circles.

"Do calm yourself, Penny," her papa warned and pulled her closer to his side.

"I am trying, Thomas. Everything must be just so." Ruby stepped up beside her mother and father just as their steward opened the large, heavily carved and polished door that reached at least ten feet high.

Mr. Bosworth, the man who had run their home as long as Ruby had been alive, opened the door and bowed slightly before stepping aside to let the man in. Ruby blinked twice and shook her head, not at all expecting the man who had just walked through the door. She knew a few guests would be arriving for the meal, but nobody ever informed Ruby in advance of the guest list.

"Is that—"

"Callum Campbell, yes," her mother whispered and looked straight ahead at the dark-haired man whose long locks were tied back in a queue beneath his black tricorn hat. He was large. Larger than she would have ever expected, though she had heard tales of his travels and adventures on the high seas as one of Scotland's fiercest pirates. It was said he did not mix with polite company much, yet he wore perfectly tailored black breeches and a leather surcoat over a crisp white tunic that no commoner could ever afford to keep so clean.

"But… Pa…" Ruby stuttered as quietly as possible so as not to be overheard. "You do not mix with his sort."

"He is wealthy, feared, capable, and has connections. Good for business. Now, do be quiet," he mumbled just as Callum stepped up to them wearing a bright smile she would never expect from such a man, the dark stubble on his chin emphasizing his strong jaw, speaking of a man who was refined enough to shave yet too rebellious to bother while dining with gentry.

"'Tis a fine home ye have, Sir Berry," Callum Campbell said with a thick Scottish brogue that made Ruby tingle all over. The Scots were heathens, everyone knew that. And a Scottish pirate? Why, he would be considered the lowest of the low. Yet here he was, at their manor right here in Cornwall where the sea surrounded them on three sides.

Removing his hat, Callum looked at her mother and then straight at her, those piercing yellow-green eyes, similar to the Spanish olives she had once delighted in, capturing her gaze as a smirk spread across his face. "And an even finer family, I see."

Penelope tittered and giggled, but Ruby just concentrated on breathing and doing her best to not look affected by the man.

Full of his usual bluster and pride, her papa puffed out his chest and stepped forward. "You are too kind! Too kind! We welcome you to our home, Lord Campbell!"

"Lord?" Ruby asked much louder than anticipated, and she took a deep breath when his eyes landed on her once more.

"Aye. Lord Argyll, if ye please," the pirate said, taking her gloved hand in his and bringing it to his lips.

"He is from a most prestigious family, my dear," her papa proclaimed, and she pursed her lips. No wonder this particular pirate was welcome in their home. Nothing she had heard about Callum Campbell spoke of him being a gentleman. Yet, he clearly had status and riches, which endeared him to her father who usually only mixed with men who were in the Queen's favor... though clearly there were exceptions. Although, she did find the man rather exceptional, herself.

Another bang on the door made Ruby jump out of her skin and her thoughts, gasping slightly and placing her gloved hand on her bosom. She noticed Lord Campbell's eyes shift down to where her hand rested, covering the tops of her exposed creamy breasts and she dared to raise a brow and narrow her eyes, making certain he was well and caught. A sly smile flashed across his face, and he winked before turning around to see who had just arrived.

Stomach plummeting as she recalled who else was to attend the dinner, Ruby made a sour face when Bosworth opened the door and she saw William standing there, looking as stiff as a board, yet smiling warmly. Greeting the Vice-Admiral, Bosworth took his hat, stepping aside as William smiled widely and walked over to her family. He passed Callum as if he was not even present, bowing politely to Thomas before kissing Penelope's hand as she lightly giggled. Ruby stood still yet did her best to smile, knowing she looked utterly ridiculous, like one of those painted masquerade masks with the forced grins.

"My dearest Ruby. How is my betrothed this evening?" She did not particularly care for the way he emphasized the word, nor the salacious way he looked at her breasts. Why it should excite her when Callum did it, yet repulsed her when her fiancé did, she could not know, nor did she care to think about it.

"Vice-Admiral," she said, giving him a small curtsy, wishing to be done with this night. Wishing she was free to live as she wished, to have adventures on the high seas as all her ancestors had done before her. Oh, she could be at sea with William, but there would be nothing but floating from one destination to the other. No capturing of ships or plundering of cargo. No rush from gaining riches while disabling an enemy ship.

10

"Shall we all find our way to the dining hall?" Thomas asked when Bosworth signaled to him that the meal was ready to begin and he put a hand out to lead the way.

Nodding, the men followed in her father's wake but she did not miss the way Callum and William looked at one another as they strode side by side. Both were tall enough, but Callum was easily two inches taller and most certainly more muscle than William.

"Do not slouch," her mother chided quietly as they entered the dining hall, and Ruby did her best to stand tall and not roll her eyes. "Do not fidget, either."

"I do not fidget!" Ruby hissed. Finding her place at the dining table, elegantly laid out with white linens, a large floral arrangement in the center and fine silver plates set out for each guest, William came over and pulled her chair out with a flourish just before she sat and nodded her thanks. While William took the seat to her left, she shot him a scathing look that nobody else seemed to notice. She was surprised to see Callum take the seat directly across from her, but not before also helping her mother to her seat at one end of the table.

Why was Callum here, and why did he and William appear to dislike one another? She knew very well why William must be here, but Callum felt like an odd addition to the table, even for a family of pirates whose manor house was close enough to the Falmouth harbor to host all sorts of strange acquaintances of her father.

"What brings you to Cornwall, Lord Campbell?" Ruby asked, folding her hands in front of her so as not to fidget. Her mother's wide grin told her she knew precisely why Ruby kept her hands where she did. It was no fun being predictable.

"A little business. A lot of pleasure," he said with a small grin, and she felt herself blushing under his keen scrutiny. He unnerved her in an exciting way and excitement was rarely found in her life as of late. Her mother and father did their best to keep her out of the family business, but all they were doing was stifling her soul and making certain William continued the job for the rest of her boring life.

Gripping her hand on the tabletop so everyone could see, William gave her a forced smile and looked at Callum. "You take a risk being here, Lord Argyll."

"What is life without a little risk, aye?" Callum replied just as the servants brought out the ewer and basin for him to wash his hands in while another brought him a drying cloth. Loaves of bread arrived just as plates of lamb and fish were set before them, both covered in a savory sauce that made Ruby's mouth water as their aromas drifted to her nose. She always wished to eat more than was polite, and her mother would scold her if she wished for more than she was given.

"I do suppose that is true. However, risks that involve your neck hanging from a noose are better off avoided." William gripped Ruby's hand tighter and she felt him shift his leg beneath the table, intentionally rubbing against hers.

"All is well, William," her father reassured before tearing into a loaf of bread. "You understand our family business and with whom we work. Callum is our guest while in Cornwall, and we trust that for the sake of our daughter, you will not cause trouble." He was so calm and confident in his position with the queen and the power he had amassed that Ruby felt a sense of pride as his daughter. Yet she still wished her papa would allow her into the family business instead of attempting to keep her out by marrying her to a man who appeared to be as straight as an arrow with his dealings.

"Indeed," William said, giving a stiff nod and a forced smile to Ruby before his gaze drifted to her breasts once more, perhaps reminding himself of why he needed to behave. The man's clammy hands and suddenly cool demeanor did not match with the warmth he had radiated in the past. Though she had never basked in his light, until now, she had at least always felt its presence.

As the meal wore on, Ruby silently listened to the men discussing business and Callum sharing tales of some of his adventures, making Ruby wish more than anything to see new lands for herself and experience more in life than hosting dinners and all the other mundane experiences she will no doubt have as the Vice-Admiral's wife. Callum's brogue had Ruby in a daze, and she watched his mouth intently while he spoke. Something about his plump lower lip and unusually straight teeth made her wonder what it would be like to kiss him.

"Isn't that right, Ruby?" she heard her father say and she shook her head, realizing she had been staring at Callum for an obscene amount of time. William cleared his throat beside her, and when she dared to look him in the eye, his displeasure was evident.

Looking back at Callum, she saw a wicked glint in his eye that told her he knew she was drawn to him. Turning to her father and taking a deep breath, Ruby shook her head, not knowing what he had asked.

"I was discussing your love of the animals. You have saved quite a few in your time. Why, just a sennight ago a bird had fallen from his nest and broken his wing. Ruby has been nursing him back to health since then. She has saved a few dogs and even a horse!"

"Yes," she replied, still snapping out of her daze. "Yes, I do quite like animals. They are innocent and dependent on our goodwill, are they not?"

"Well, I find it uncouth and hope that will not continue once you are my wife. A Vice-Admiral's wife does not bring diseased, flea-ridden beasts into their home."

Ruby scowled at William for saying such ridiculous nonsense, but the man was too busy using his finger to pick out a chunk of meat from his teeth to notice.

"I agree," her mother said with a firm nod and a titter. "I have told her as much since the day she was born but alas, the child cannot stop coddling those beasts."

Ruby wanted to bang her head on a wall, or better yet, dig her nails into the fine linens covering the table, but instead, she looked straight ahead at the raised brow of Callum Campbell who seemed to listen and observe, yet thankfully not audibly share his distaste.

"Well, my Ruby has a kind heart," her father said as an afterthought, and despite her displeasure at this arranged marriage to this pompous man, she did quite love and cherish her father for always doing what he thought was best for her. If only she were allowed an opinion on the matter.

"Would we care to retire to the hall for some cards?" Papa asked, thankfully changing the subject, and once everyone had washed their hands again with the ewer and pitcher, they stood from their seats, following Bosworth to their next location, as if they did not already know where to find their own hall.

Ceremony bored Ruby to tears. Truly she just wished to go check on Hera, the small bird she had saved, then retire before William attempted to kiss her once more. After the last family meal, he had cornered her and demanded a kiss, and though it was not an unpleasant one to be fair, it had been unnatural and obligatory—not at all how she would prefer it.

The Vice-Admiral was not the first man Ruby had ever kissed, but he had been the oldest. Sharing kisses with the stable lad when her father wasn't around had been a secret adventure Ruby had rather enjoyed before becoming betrothed to William.

Fortunately, William proceeded past her on their way to the hall, clearly in a rush to monopolize her father's conversation before Callum could, which suited Ruby just fine, while Mama walked alongside them both, enraptured by whatever nonsense they spoke of.

Suddenly, something jerked her back and she almost gasped, but a strong hand came over her mouth and she felt herself being dragged around a corner before feeling the wall against her back. Widening her eyes, she looked at Callum, who stood only a few inches away and several inches above her, his olive eyes shifting as they searched her face. "Ye would do well to learn not to stare at other men while your husband sits beside ye, lass."

Pulling his hand off her mouth, Ruby shoved at him, but Callum felt like a solid wall of muscle pinned against her. Fear should have consumed her, but all she could feel was excitement and a tightening in her belly. "He is not my husband. And I was not staring at you!" she huffed with indignation.

"Only one of those statements is true, lass," he said as he waggled his brows. "He will be yer husband and he is a man of import to ye English, aye? I ken what ye want. I see it in yer eyes. But ye cannae have it, not with him at yer side."

"Oh, and what is it you *ken* I want?" she asked, trying her best to sound like a Scot.

"Adventure. And perhaps a real man. But ye ken ye willnae have either, so best ye keep yer eyes on the man ye will marry and forget yer own desires."

With that, Callum moved away from her, turning to leave the room as she panted against the wall, wondering what had just happened and why she felt as if she may lose her bearings. "Pirate?" she called just before he disappeared around the corner.

"Aye?" Turning around, she saw his eyes squinting at her even in the darkness, their glowing yellow-green too brilliant to be snuffed out by the lack of lighting.

"Would you take such advice from another? Would you give up all you wanted because others had decided what was best for you?"

Propping an arm against the wall, he smiled knowingly at her and shook his head. "I think ye already ken the answer to that," he winked, pretending to tip the hat he no longer wore on his head before walking away.

Pushing herself off the wall, Ruby brushed her blonde hair off her shoulders and straightened her spine, narrowing her deep blue eyes.

"Precisely."

Chapter 2

Cards were not his favorite pastime. He preferred standing at the helm of his ship and watching the water rush past, smelling the sea and salt in the thick air, feeling his long dark hair being controlled by the wind. He also enjoyed the feel of a bonnie wee lass beneath him, and suddenly one face, in particular, flashed in his mind.

Propped up against the wall of the hall, Callum watched as William and Thomas played cards while Penelope Berry sat in a chair with her needlework. Observing people was his specialty. He could read them, see into them, know their secrets. And while William Stanhope was a man with darkness swimming in the irises of his brown eyes that Callum had unfortunately witnessed in the past, Ruby Berry was a woman still innocent, seeking things in life she would never have, certainly not with William, anyway.

He had meant to warn her, to chase her off his scent, to make her see that her fate had already been assigned to her.

Yet, when he stood over her, felt her heavy breathing against his neck, he knew she would never resign herself. She was a wild mare deep in her soul. Blonde hair and blue eyes could not hide the desire for more than she was allowed to seek. Her family had been privateers for generations, nobles who smuggled or plundered for the crown, keeping a fair share for themselves, protected by their royal counterparts. They were gentlemen pirates who stuck to a code, glorified pirates with estates and manors and titles… and bonnie daughters who they wished to keep away from the dangers of their existence.

But Callum was not a privateer. He plundered for nobody but himself and his men. Scotland owed nothing to the bloody Queen of England who suppressed the royal house of Stuart for their own greed. Nay. Callum may be noble-born, the Earl of Argyll, but he was no gentleman, nor did he pretend to be… unlike a certain man in this room who hid his secrets well from the likes of Sir Thomas Berry.

Coming to Cornwall had been unpleasant, yet necessary. Few people knew of Thomas Berry's sympathies to the Stuarts and while he would never openly betray his queen, who allowed him to plunder her enemies as he saw fit, he had recently come across some stolen Stuart family jewels and wished to keep them in the hands of the Scottish monarchs, even if oppressed. Callum may be a bloody pirate, but he was loyal to his people and vowed to retrieve the jewels and see them safely back to his land. Aye, he had known he would be dining with Thomas's daughter and her fiancé, but he had not known she was betrothed to the grandest bastard in all the world, nor had he been prepared for the likes of Ruby Berry.

Named after his favorite gemstone, she was a treasure all her own. It was not simply her alabaster breasts or how well they would fill his palms, nor the way she nervously bit on her plush pink lips as she stared at him from across the table, with eyes the same color blue as the Mediterranean sky during the summer months. There was more to the lass than a bonnie face. She had intelligence, wit, ambition, a will to do more in this life than simply exist and sit in a chair with her needlework. She had goals, and though it went against the grain to stifle such desires, it was not his place to encourage them. And one day, that glimmer he had seen in her eyes would get her into more trouble than she could handle.

"Where is Ruby?" Penelope asked, finally looking up from her needlework.

"Likely, she has retired early," her father said as he examined the cards in his hand.

"Just as well," William sighed, placing a card down on the table. "She would only have protested when we informed her of the news."

Callum shifted his stance and popped his knuckles, finally speaking for the first time since entering the room. "What news?"

"None of your concern, pirate." William scoffed incredulously and continued to stare at his cards. Callum squinted his eyes and popped his knuckles again, remembering the knife stuffed in his boot and itching to slice open the man's throat with it.

"Ruby and William are set to marry in a sennight. Unfortunately, he has business in London and must sail there at dawn, taking Ruby with him," Thomas explained.

"She will not be pleased," Penelope added. "Yet as the Vice-Admiral's wife, she will learn that she goes where she is needed."

He could not understand why, but something inside him clenched and his anger threatened to explode. Why did he feel protective of a woman he had only known for a matter of hours? Perhaps it was because she had spirit and a fire in her veins that he felt simmering beneath the surface. Perhaps he simply saw a lot of himself in her, the need for more than a stuffy life inside a manor home.

Looking at William with his upturned nose, and the scowl he shot across the room from time to time, only heightened Callum's scorn. The man was scum, and after what he had done to Callum's family in the past, he deserved little more than death. How was a treasure such as Ruby meant to spend her life with the bastard?

It was only his respect for Sir Thomas Berry that had prevented Callum from killing William already. Callum took a deep breath and watched the men play cards before a low hissing sound caught his ear. At first, it sounded like steam escaping a pot, but the sound was coming from behind the door frame. Nodding to his hosts, Callum discreetly excused himself to follow the sound, not having much else to do with himself aside from thinking far more about Ruby than was healthy.

Once around the corner and engulfed by the darkness, Callum saw a flickering light turn a corner of the corridor ahead. Squinting, he decided to follow, knowing that whatever it was, it was far more interesting than the two men playing cards and the older woman stitching a canvas. He was used to merry-making with his men, drinking ale, and chasing skirts. Formal parties other than his own had always bored him to tears. But dark hallways and flickering lights always held the promise of a secret.

Rounding the corner, Callum stopped abruptly when he bumped into a wee golden-haired lass wearing naught more than a shift that looked as transparent as gossamer in the light of the candle she held in one hand. Her other hand reached up to her plump lips, signaling him to be quiet before she turned expecting him to follow.

Devil's bollocks. He had seen more of the lass than he had ever expected and now, all he could imagine was removing her finely made shift, tossing it to the floor, and showing her how a pirate made love to a woman. Following in her wake, Callum watched the curve of her backside as she walked barefooted down yet another corridor of this mansion she had been so coddled in for her entire twenty years of life. He was only five and twenty yet had seen more of the world than most men would see in a full lifetime, and the thought of allowing her to experience it, as well, made him smirk into the darkness while she turned toward a room, opening the door.

As soon as he followed her in, Ruby shut the door behind him, and he turned to face her, lowering his brow. "'Tis dangerous to lure pirates down dark corridors, lass."

Raising a brow, Ruby held the candle in front of her body and met his gaze. "I do not fear you. I know you do not wish to harm me."

"Och, lass. Nay, that is not what I wish to do with ye."

"Oh? Oh!" she squeaked when she caught on to his meaning, but she did not back up, nor shrink in fear. "That is unexpected."

"Is it? Ye are a bonnie lass. Ye ken that. Ye must." Callum stared at her and swore he saw a blush creeping across her cheeks, but perhaps it was a trick of the light.

"I most certainly do not," she huffed.

"No man has ever told ye that ye are bonnie?" he asked, stepping closer and pushing a blonde ringlet behind her ear. "No man has ever kissed ye? Or… touched ye?" he asked slowly. "Ye ken I willnae judge ye. I am called the Scourge of the Seas, not the saint."

Again, she did not pull back. When she licked her lips, he wanted to groan, to lean in and taste her. "I have shared a few kisses. Not more," she said proudly and he smiled at her courage.

"Have ye kissed the Vice-Admiral?" Callum was intrigued. She was full of life. A repressed spirit clearly straining to be released, and William seemed to be the wet cloth waiting to snuff out her flame. He did not deserve Ruby, and now that Thomas Berry had been seen feasting with a Scottish pirate, he was in danger.

All she did was nod and frown, and that was all he needed to see to know she had not wanted, nor enjoyed it. "Why did ye lure me into this room, Ruby?" He liked the sound of her name on his lips, but he would prefer the sound of her moans while she writhed against his face. That visual made him clench his jaw and fight back urges he knew he had to control.

"I overheard the discussion in the hall," she replied flatly. "I know they plan to awaken me on the morrow with packed bags so they can toss me aboard his ship and send me away to my new life. I am seething with rage," she ground out. "I do not deserve such a fate!"

"Now that, we can agree on, lass."

"You do?" she asked, surprise in her tone.

"Aye. But, what is it ye want from me, lass? Because I dinnae believe ye want from me what I want from ye."

"I... I..." She stuttered and froze, a definite blush now creeping over her cheeks. "I do not know, exactly."

Rubbing his lips together, he stared at the woman for a moment, considering his options. If she were not a maiden, he would be tempted to persuade her to remove her shift and allow him to taste the sweet rosebuds he had seen through the fabric only moments earlier. But, she was innocent and he did not chase maidens, especially betrothed ones.

"Allow me to make ye a proposal," he said slowly, raising a brow and was amused by the slight indignation that contorted her face. Laughing loudly, he felt her hand cover his mouth as she frowned.

"Do be quiet. If we are caught, I am ruined."

"Would that be so bad? Then ye would be forced to marry me. Even I ken I am better than that cold English fish."

"You… would marry me?" she asked and slowly put the candlestick down on a table against the wall.

Snorting, Callum put his hands up in the air and took a step back. "Och, nay. Nay, I am not a man ye would want fer a husband, lass. Even if ye were ruined, I would sail away before dawn, before being forced to marry." Her face fell and she put her hands on her hips, clearly insulted by his honestly. "Listen, lass. It isnae ye. I have never wished to marry and shall never do so."

"Then what is it you propose, pirate? And do know I will scream if you attempt anything."

"I do believe ye are the one who brought me here, lass. But, I offer ye this: Yer fiancé's ship leaves at dawn whether ye are on it or nay."

"What are you saying?" she asked, listening intently and appearing intrigued.

"I am merely stating a fact. If by some chance ye are missing or unable to be found by dawn, he will be forced to sail without ye. His queen willnae wait."

"Are you saying you will kidnap me?"

"Ye really do think I am a fool, dinnae ye?" When she didn't answer, he shook his head and stepped closer to her so he could speak softly in case any staff should wander into the room. "I dinnae ken where ye would hide. But as far as they ken, ye dinnae ken ye must leave at dawn, aye? Perhaps ye left for a long ride? His ship will sail off and ye will arrive home, dismayed to discover that yer love has sailed away without ye."

"He is not my love," she protested and moved further into the room and away from the flame that had allowed him to see her features. Though they were mostly in the shadows, he could still see her slight silhouette.

"I sense the wildness in ye, lass. I ken ye want to live, to have an adventure. I can relate to that. I dinnae ken why I feel compelled to help ye, but I will. It is yer choice to make and the first of many if ye allow me to take ye to London for yer wedding."

Her face soured, and she plopped on a couch he had not even known was there in the darkness. Slowly lowering himself, he sat beside her and whispered in her ear. "I cannae change yer fate. I cannae stop yer wedding. But I can stay back on the morrow and be ready to escort ye to London. Once aboard my ship, I will allow ye to have free will until we reach our destination. I warn ye. 'Tis a pirate ship and the men are a wild lot. Ye will need to stay close to me, under my protection, but if ye take my offer—"

Her lips crashed down on his and he froze, unmoving, unsure if he should pull away or deepen it. Against his instincts and his desires, Callum pulled away and looked at Ruby, who frowned. "Why did ye do that?"

"I was making my first decision," she whispered, leaning in once more.

Placing his hands on either side of her face, he held her still, surprised how soft and smooth her creamy skin felt against his warm, calloused hands. "We arenae aboard the ship yet," he reminded her, arching a brow and searching her face. By the devil's bollocks, she was a temping lass. He considered that he perhaps had made a mistake in offering to give her an adventure. He was not so certain he would turn away a toss in the sheets if she begged for it. The thought of Ruby on her knees begging him to undress her made him go hard as a rod, and he cursed himself for the lecher he was.

"I want to kiss you, Callum. Please? I wish to see how it feels. Kissing William felt like kissing a distant cousin. Not entirely inappropriate but disgusting all the same. Are kisses supposed to feel that way?" she asked, cocking her head. "I have kissed the stable lad a few times and it was better for certain, but still, nothing as exciting as I had expected."

Callum observed this woman before him, so innocent yet clearly built for sin. And he considered it a sin that those lips should be used for mediocre kisses. The temptation was strong. Too strong to resist. She smelled sweet and floral and the image of her nipples showing through her shift consumed him.

Leaning in, he took her lips with his, starting slow and languid, savoring the moment, knowing it would be the only time he allowed such a thing to occur between them. She wanted to see if it felt like kissing a cousin? He would make certain she knew the difference. Her soft lips parted and she hesitated, unsure how far he was going to take this kiss. He was unsure, as well. Should he stop before he took things too far? He was not a man used to stopping after a wee kiss.

But the small groan that escaped her sweet lips was the beginning of the end. His undoing. Her innocence was not a trait he was used to in a woman, and yet, he found it drove him wild. Pulling her closer, Callum wrapped his hands around her waist and pulled her onto his lap. She squeaked but did not break contact as his tongue slipped between her lips, stroking hers at first lightly, teasingly, before increasing the pressure. Her hands gripped his shoulders and dug into his flesh, her breasts brushing against his chest.

He wanted her. He wanted all of her. So badly that he was certain she could feel the evidence of his need pressing against her belly but she did not seem to mind, not even after he lost control of his better senses and pulled her down against him, feeling her through the thin shift. Ruby squirmed and he groaned, and he was ready to pull his breeches down to his thighs, pull her shift up to her waist, and sheath himself in her wet heat. Take her maidenhead.

That thought finally broke through to what little sense he had left in his lust-crazed mind. She was a maiden, betrothed to a Vice-Admiral of the queen who would make merry and drink fine French wine while his neck dangled from a noose before her. William would potentially beat her if he found out she was no maiden.

Pulling away and panting while he regained control, Callum pressed his forehead against hers and gave her one more soft kiss, the last he would ever allow. "Was that like kissing yer cousin, lass?"

He heard her swallow before she responded, felt her breasts heaving, and saw her lick her lips. "N-no. No, it was not." Slowly sliding off his lap, he felt her body quivering and he wasn't sure if it was from need or shock. He was shocked, himself.

He may be a pirate, but he used better judgment in most situations. He had to. One wrong move could mean his death on any day. Yet, his instinct was to pull her close once more, and he cursed his weakness for a bonnie face. That's all this was. She affected him with lust. Whatever else he was feeling was simply driven by his attraction.

Adjusting himself, he saw her eyes widen at the bulge in his breeches, but he paid her no mind. What did the woman think would happen when she pulled him into a dark room wearing nothing more than a transparent shift and begged to be kissed? "Now, get ye off to bed before ye are caught with me and I have to kill yer betrothed at dawn. If ye wish to sail with him on the morrow, then this is goodbye, and I wish ye well, sweet Ruby. If ye wish to take me up on the offer of adventure on the high seas, then I leave a plan up to ye."

Standing up, Callum tipped his head to the young English woman who made him lose his senses and turned to leave the room, heading back to his ship and his men for the night. Mayhap he could find a willing serving lass to ease his discomfort and take his mind off Ruby.

Part of him hoped she took his offer, yet most of him prayed she decided to get on that ship with William at dawn. He had not stood seven minutes alone with the lass before nearly ripping her clothes off and burying himself inside her. How would he last several days?

Ruby Berry was a temptress of the highest order, and worst of all, she did not even know it. And of all the rubies he had possessed in his lifetime, he knew without a doubt that she was the finest treasure a man would find, for no gem or gold coin could shine as bright as she.

Chapter 3

Sleep was impossible. With the light's reflection flickering off her walls from the candle that still burned on her side table, Ruby laid on her back and stared up at the ceiling, trying to absorb the events of the night starting from the very moment Callum Campbell had entered her home. Never had she reacted to a man so viscerally. It was like her entire world had stopped yet spun at the same time while her breath left and had yet to return.

And that kiss. She wanted to regret it, to feel guilty for kissing a man who was not William, and yet, how could one regret such a profound moment in life, learning that physical interactions with a man could feel like more than routine, awkward moments. Callum had made her feel small, yet strong, feminine yet capable. He gave her a choice and when she made it, he did not turn her down. She believed he would have and had meant to, yet for some reason, had decided to humor her. After all, that's all it had been, right? A well-experienced man humoring an innocent lass' desire to discover. Besides, it had only been a kiss and naught more.

The memory of his hard length pressing against her sensitive flesh when he pulled her on his lap made her quake, despite the warm covers that engulfed her. Humor or not, he had enjoyed that kiss and believed her to be a bonnie lass, as the Scottish said.

Dawn was fast approaching and Ruby needed to make a decision. Indignation and melancholy plagued her, that her parents would simply ship her off without warning. Her wedding had been planned, she knew, even if nobody felt the need to give her the details. Perhaps they thought she would seek an escape if she knew when it was to occur. Yet, never had she thought to be shipped away, married in London to a man she hardly knew without them in attendance.

Papa loved her; this she knew well. He meant to protect her from what he saw as a wild and reckless spirit she had owned the entirety of her life. But the blood of pirates ran through her veins. Fire. Strong will. Defiance. She was not born to be a restrained woman and he knew this. Instead of accepting her for who she was, he wished to control her by marrying her to a man who would intentionally break her spirit.

The more Ruby laid in bed and stared at the dying flames of the candle, the more angry and defiant she became. Would she spend the rest of her life with William? Yes, she would. But could she take a final opportunity to have the adventure her heart sought? Would she regret it for the rest of her life if she did not take the chance? She already knew the answers.

Closing her eyes, she could still feel Callum's grip on her waist, feel her breasts pressed against his strong chest, his heavy breathing, and the way her body melted against his. She would never feel that again, not with William and certainly not with Callum, for she had to use all her strength to prevail against her strong attraction to the man. If she decided to go with him, she would have to promise not to touch him or ask for another earth-shattering kiss. It would do no good to further torture herself.

Hopping out of bed, Ruby swiped her hands down her face, exhausted yet restless. Sleep was an impossibility and by the glow permeating her window, dawn was upon her. Stay or go. Go or stay. Now was time to decide. She would either disappoint her parents or disappoint herself and neither felt like a fair option, but nobody had ever considered what was fair to her.

Either way, she needed to be dressed before her maid came to turn down her sheets and yank on her curls with that horrid metal comb. Running to her bureau, Ruby scanned her options and picked a comfortable green linen dress that she could manage to tie up herself, even if it was poorly done.

Spinning circles in her room for a moment, Ruby went to the door and back to her desk, and back to the door again. "Curse it!" she groaned and plopped on the bed, hastily donning her stockings and riding boots, then draping her cloak around her shoulders. She was not going to London with William. Never had she consented to do so, nor had she even been told so. Opening the door slowly, Ruby stifled a scream when she was met with a pair of dark brown eyes surrounded by wrinkles of flesh.

"Oh! Gerty, you frightened me," Ruby whispered, placing her hand over her beating heart.

"I have come to get ye ready for the day, mistress. As always," Gertrude replied, looking slightly irritated. Her maid was extremely old. Much too old to even be working still, or even standing, yet somehow the old woman got up every day before the sun and was usually kind enough, if not a tad stern. But, she was loyal and would keep to herself and Ruby valued that quality above all others just now.

"Yes, I know, thank you, Gerty. I could not sleep and thought to go for a ride. I have dressed myself as you can see." The old maid wrinkled her already wrinkled nose, clearly not approving of Ruby's appearance, but that did not matter.

"I cannae let ye out looking like that. Master will think I have lost me wits and sack me!"

"Nonsense," Ruby soothed, placing a hand on the woman's frail shoulder. "You will turn around now and simply say when you came to my room, I was already gone. In fact, I beg you to give me a quarter hour's head start before you run to Papa and say I have gone missing."

Narrowing her dark bushy brows, Gertrude's nostrils flared. "Has this anything to do with that Mister Stanhope coming to visit ye?"

"What?" Ruby played innocent, doing her best to sound offended. "Absolutely not. He is my betrothed, after all. I have no reason to avoid him. I simply cannot sleep and wished to ride for a bit before breaking my fast. I trust this is acceptable and you will simply tell Papa I am nowhere to be found. I will return, I vow. I simply do not wish to be found until I am ready to be."

Pursing her lips, Gertrude shrugged and huffed a deep breath murmuring something about it being Ruby's hide, not hers, and shuffling down the hall.

Breathing deeply, Ruby shut her door carefully and ran down the stairs before reaching the hall, looking around the room. Bosworth was busy as usual, bossing people about in the dining area. Of course, she would not truly ride, she only meant for it to appear that way. Ruby took the opportunity to tiptoe over to the library where she had every intention of simply hiding like a small child beneath the desk where Papa rarely sat. Nobody would be in the room for hours. Once the house realized she was missing, the first thing Papa would do was ride out to find her and drag her back to William's ship, but she would be nowhere to be found.

Sitting beneath the musty wooden desk with her knees tucked up, she laughed at herself for looking so foolish. But, freedom had its price and she was willing to pay it. Within a few moments, she heard the commotion start, and she pursed her lips and cupped her mouth with her hand.

"What do you mean Ruby was not in her room?" she heard Papa holler as he stormed down the stairs.

"Where could she have gone?" Mama wailed. "We never even had a chance to tell her she must leave today!"

"We must leave immediately, madam," William said with an annoyed edge, and Ruby rolled her eyes at his pompous air. "My men are ready and the weather favors us. The queen expects us on time. I cannot tarry."

"Yes, yes. We shall find her," Papa said, staying calm. "The young woman must have gone for a ride. After all, she did not know she was to leave. I have Gertrude packing her bags as we speak. I will find her and you will have time to spare, William."

"It was that damned Scottish pirate!" William spat, and his words made Ruby sit up straight beneath the table, straining to hear his words. "I saw how he was looking at her last night. He has abducted her! I will get her back!"

So, William had seen Callum's interest in her? Why did that excite Ruby? She had seen him look at her a time or two, but never did she believe it to be anything beyond curiosity.

"I am certain Callum has nothing to do with her disappearance, William. He is a guest here and knows better than to do such things. However, we could use his help. I will ride out to search the surrounding lands. Penelope and Bosworth will search the grounds. William, you go to Callum's ship and seek his help. We shall find her."

Nobody spoke after that and when the door slammed shut, Ruby settled back beneath the desk, hoping to wait for the right time to reappear, which would only happen once William was long gone.

"Capt'n!" A knock resounded on Callum's door and he cursed in frustration.

"What!" he shouted as he sat up in bed, looking down at the mass of blonde hair beside him, having no memory of the night once he left Berry Manor.

"There is an Englishman here to see ye, Capt'n!"

An Englishman? Had Thomas Berry come down here to kill him? If so, he had better make sure he was at least wearing breeches. That would be embarrassing. "Which Englishman? Does he have a name? There are so many of them." Callum said as he climbed out of bed and swiftly pulled his breeches on before cracking the door open.

Being met by the wide eyes of his second mate, he raised a brow. "Well, which one is it?"

"Ye ken," Samuel said softy so only Callum could hear. "'Tis *him*, Capt'n. The one with the bonnie bride. The one who… ye ken…"

Eyes widening, Callum scowled and pushed the door open wider. "Ye mean William Stanhope, the man responsible for my father's death. He dares set foot upon my ship?"

"Yes. That one." William stepped between the men, pushing Samuel out of the way. Callum wanted to remind the man whose ship he was on, but he was too curious as to why the man was here. "I have come looking for my Ruby."

"Och, well. Ye ken I have many rubies but they are mine, not yers. If ye want one, ye will have to ask nicely." Crossing his arms and standing in his doorway, he smiled when his crew began to laugh, and William's face turned bright red with rage.

"You know exactly which Ruby I speak of, Pirate!"

"That's Lord Argyll to ye, lad. And ye are fortunate I dinnae kill ye where ye stand as I wish to. But I assure ye, if ye ever step foot on my ship again once we leave Cornwall, I willnae hesitate.

William sputtered and pushed Callum aside. "Let me in, you piece of scum!" Callum stepped aside and leaned against the doorway while the belligerent Englishman pushed through, stopping to stare at the bed. Though he seethed inside, Callum reminded himself that killing William would not benefit him, though it would help Ruby. Perhaps another time, he decided and popped his knuckles.

Callum's gaze followed William's to the woman-sized lump beneath the sheets and he smiled widely, knowing exactly what the man believed. William stepped toward the bed, seeing a small mass of blonde hair sticking out of the top and Callum cut him off, putting a hand out. "I cannae allow ye to do that," he warned before William could pull the covers back.

"How dare you stand in my way, you heathen! Is that my betrothed beneath those sheets?"

"Nay, 'tis not, and if ye touch the lass I will break yer nose." Callum did not even remember the woman's name, but she was his guest and already being forced to hide beneath the sheets in shame. He could see her shift and squirm uncomfortably and turned to William, scowling in warning.

"Stand aside!" William drew his sword and pointed it at Callum's neck, who did nothing but stay still and continue to glower. Behind William, his first mate drew his sword and pointed it at his back, making certain the man felt its point in his spine.

"I assure ye, 'tis not yer betrothed beneath this sheet and ye are harassing the woman. Leave now before ye regret it."

"I will not until I see her face!" William shouted, yet had the sense to drop his sword at his side.

Before Callum could warn William once more, the woman sat straight up in the bed and uncovered her face before wrapping the sheet around her body. "Am I who ye are looking for, eh?" Looking him up and down, she scoffed and bent over to pick up her torn linen dress from the floor of his cabin. Callum could not remember a single detail of the night before and was glad of it when he saw her missing front teeth and odd beak-like nose. He must have drunk himself into oblivion at the alehouse after leaving Ruby the night before, and he held back a shudder. Ruby must have affected him more than he suspected, yet William was here seeking her out. That meant she had taken him up on his offer, which pleased him greatly, and not only because it angered her arse of a fiancé.

William's mouth gaped open when he looked at the woman who was not Ruby and before he could respond, the lass kicked him in the shin with her barefoot, then cracked him across the face with a right hook, making him step back in shock, sputtering a curse. Callum's eyes widened and he crossed his arms, nodding with respect.

William lunged at the woman, but Callum stepped in between and pushed him toward the door. "Ye have worn out what little welcome ye had here, Vice-Admiral. I havenae seen Ruby since the meal last night, and I will ask ye to leave now before I make ye."

Shooting daggers at the whore with his eyes, William spat a glob of blood out onto the floor and stepped past her. "I do not have time for any of this. Lord Berry will regret his daughter's poor behavior." William stormed out of the cabin where he was immediately met with the stares of dozens of pirates as he walked down the gangplank.

Turning to look at Callum, the lass flashed him a toothless smile. "I had a grand night with ye, sir pirate. Now where be me payment?"

Payment? Devil's bollocks… he had picked up a whore? He must have truly been out of his mind the night before and prayed he did nothing that would make him piss blood eventually. "Samuel, get this fine woman a shilling for her time," Callum said to his second mate, signaling for the woman to follow him out.

"A shilling?" she gasped and dropped the sheet onto the floor, exposing herself as she slipped her well-worn dress over her head without shame. "But, we dinnae even do anything!"

Callum tilted his head at her and raised a brow. "We dinnae?"

"Ye dinnae remember? Och ye fell asleep, ye did. I cannae take a shilling. I only require half that!"

Relief flooded him. He had never fallen asleep before bedding a woman, but he had never picked up a whore either. He must have been extremely inebriated to have done so before falling asleep. "Take it, miss. For yer honesty and time."

Shrugging, she followed Samuel out of the cabin, and Callum took a deep breath, running his hands through his tangled shoulder-length hair. That was one of the more interesting ways he had been awoken in his lifetime, and that was saying something. Miss Ruby Berry had a way of turning powerful men mad with possessiveness and lust. He would do well to remember this moment and take heed when dealing with the lass in the future. She was naught but trouble, and not the good kind. A man would kill to part her slim legs and taste her nectar, but he was not the man for the job.

Pulling his white tunic over his head, Callum slipped on his boots, strapped on his belt, and threw on his hat before leaving his quarters in a rush. He had to find Ruby and offer Lord Berry assistance in delivering her to London. By the light of day, Callum questioned his madness. Whatever had possessed him to plot with the likes of that siren? Perhaps the shadows had played tricks on his mind, or the wine he had been served was of a stronger variety. Surely he had lost his wits. But, he was a man of his word. He had told her he would take her on a high seas adventure, and so he would.

But, Miss Ruby Berry was untouchable. Off-limits. Betrothed to another. And surely, not as bonnie as he had remembered her to be in his lusty mind the night before. He was most certain he would look upon her face once more today and she would be as homely as the whore he had just paid for absolutely no reason other than relieving him of the worry of acquiring a foul disease.

Nay, Callum was a pirate who had sailed the world and bedded many beautiful, exotic women. There was no way he could not handle a spoiled English miss.

"I cannot handle you, Ruby!" Papa shouted when she finally reappeared from her hiding spot in the library. Having ruffled up her hair and pinched her cheeks to better appear windswept, Ruby carefully tiptoed out of the library and into the hall, pretending not to understand why everyone was in a state of frenzy.

"I do not understand, Papa. I could not sleep, so I went for a ride. I did naught wrong. You never informed me I was meant to leave at dawn. And, I am angry at *you* for trying to ship me off with no warning!" she spat, putting her hands on her hips. She may be play-acting, but her hurt feelings were genuine.

"I went to the stables and your horse was still there!" he shouted back and Ruby blanched, not having thought of such details.

"I... I took a different horse! Did you check all the stalls?" she said, sticking to her story and praying he backed down.

"No... no, I did not," he sighed, and his shoulders sagged. "I do not know what to do now. I am sorry, Ruby. We meant to tell you after the meal last night, but you disappeared to bed, and William could not tarry. Now, what are we to do?"

"I can take her."

All eyes turned to look at the man who seemed to have simply appeared from the shadows, and Ruby's heart leaped into her throat when she spotted him. He was so tall and regal, clearly noble-born by the way he carried himself, yet he had an edge and a roughness about him that bespoke of a man well-traveled and a bit rebellious. And his brogue would never stop making her tingle from head to toe, she vowed, remembering how it sounded against her ear last night when he moved her onto his lap and kissed her like a man kisses a lover. Feeling her cheeks turning pink, Ruby looked away just as his olive-green eyes turned to her, and she looked back at her father.

"Callum. I did not hear you enter," Thomas said, holding Penelope's hand.

"I am sorry to intrude. Ye see, I had a visit from the Vice-Admiral. He was in a rage, searching for Ruby upon my ship. When he found no trace of her, he was verra angry and said ye will regret it. I warn ye, Sir Berry. He kens ye do business with a Scot now. William may give ye trouble, he doesnae like pirates."

Ruby bit her bottom lip and looked at her father as he turned red with bluster, not at all accustomed to being threatened and, not for the first time, she wondered why he wished to marry her to such a man. "I know he does not. But, he loves Ruby and will never cause me trouble, I am certain. Besides, I have letters of marque from the queen. I am a privateer, not a pirate," Papa stressed, and Ruby did her best not to roll her eyes. He convinced nobody but himself.

Callum stepped forward and stopped next to Ruby, looking down at her shrewdly before looking back at her father. Ruby's stomach flipped just being so close to him. Why did he excite her so much? She had better control herself if she was to be with the man for several days… assuming her papa accepted Callum's offer.

"I am on my way north. It would be no trouble at all to bring her to the port near London. From there, she can find an escort to find William. I can have her there safely and with time to spare. 'Tis only a few days' journey."

Her papa rubbed his chin and looked at her mama, who nodded emphatically in support of the idea, which shocked Ruby. "Oh, yes. We must get Ruby to Westminster on time. We simply must, Thomas. Or else William will be displeased."

Thomas looked at Callum, scrutinizing him with his eyes. "Can I trust you with my daughter's virtue, Lord Argyll? I will call on your honor as a nobly born man to see my daughter safely to London, and I expect her to remain chaste."

"Papa!" Ruby scolded, humiliation coursing through her blood.

"Ye have my word," Callum said with a nod.

"You will keep her safe. I do not like the idea of Ruby aboard a pirate's ship. It is the very thing I have fought to avoid these many years, and why I have arranged for her to marry a man who will keep her on a straight path. I would take her myself but gathering a crew and preparing for the journey would simply take too much time."

"Papa…" Ruby began to point out his hypocrisy, to remind him that he was both a gentleman pirate and married to a good woman who had remained out of trouble, but also that she was smart enough to make her own choices. However, he put out a staying hand and stepped closer to her.

"Ruby. My sweet Ruby. I know you have been angry with me. I know you have the spirit of your ancestors. I see the twinkle in your eye, and that is what scares me. You will always be my greatest treasure and nothing could ever change that." Leaning in, he kissed her forehead and placed his large hands on her shoulders. The sincerity in his eyes made her tear up, but she choked them back, refusing to cry now for the first time in her memory. "Do recall your departed cousin, and why I must keep you safe. Please do not be angry with me for the decisions I have made. Perhaps traveling with Lord Argyll will satisfy the need for adventure you crave and give you time to accept your reality as William's wife."

"Oh, Ruby!" Shrieking like a banshee, her mother ran toward her, embracing her tighter than ever before. "Do behave. Do not slouch or fidget. Remember your manners. And please, be safe." Ruby rolled her eyes but hugged her mother back, looking up at Callum who fought back his amusement.

"I will have your luggage sent to the ship. I trust Callum with your safety." Her father nodded at Callum and looked back at her. "I will see you before the autumn, my little treasure. You will be a married woman when next I lay eyes on you." Her father hugged her, and Ruby lost control. A floodgate of tears ran down her cheeks as she squeezed her father with all she had. She was angry and frustrated that they had taken away all her choices in life, but she loved them dearly and knew they only did what they thought was best. Her father was trusting her to travel aboard a pirate ship and that alone made up for many of his errors.

Still, Ruby was on her way to London to marry a man she could hardly tolerate on his best day and that idea loomed in her mind like a black cloud blotting out the sun. Looking back at Callum, who gave her a secret wink, her spirits lifted slightly. They had plotted together and they had succeeded. And soon, they would be aboard his ship and she would be free for several days to do as she wished before becoming the Vice-Admiral's stifled wife. But, until then, she was as free as a bird with only the horizon as her limit.

Chapter 4

Every man aboard the ship stared as Ruby walked up the gangplank, and Callum scowled a warning at them all. This idea had seemed better by night with several glasses of wine in his blood and with Ruby in a transparent gown. Now, she was dressed like a Baron's daughter, regally stepping onto a ship full of pirates in the early morning light as a line of servants walked behind them, carrying her belongings.

Escorting her to his quarters, Callum opened the door and stepped aside so the servants could drop off her bags and leave. Ruby looked up at him with confusion in her eyes. "I am staying in the captain's quarters?"

"Aye."

"Alone?"

"Nay." Callum crossed his arms and raised a brow. "This is a ship, lass. Not an inn. I dinnae have spare rooms, so unless ye wish to sleep below with the men, this will have to do."

"Oh. Right. Of course." Ruby fidgeted, her fingers playing with the lengths of her silk skirt that matched the blue of her eyes. Her cheeks were rosy from the wind whipping her face on the journey down to the harbor and her curls were slightly disheveled, yet still somehow regal. One thing was for certain: Ruby Berry was a brilliant star among dull grains of sand on this ship and he was not so certain he had considered this well enough.

"I will sleep on the bed?" she asked, looking around the sparsely appointed room containing little more than a bed built into the wall, a desk where he kept his papers, one small side table, and a chest filled with his belongings.

"Aye, I had assumed so."

"And you will sleep…"

"I havenae figured that out yet." Callum sighed and did his best to remind himself that this was his idea. He had wanted to give her an adventure before becoming married to that arse of a man. She was more than a spoiled English lass, though. He saw it then, and he saw it now. He could do this. It was only a few days and he had slept in far worse conditions. He could sleep on his cabin's floor or with the crew if necessary. "Settle in and prepare for the journey. I need to instruct my men."

Walking out of his cabin, Callum let out a whistle loud enough to make every member of his crew stop in their tracks and look straight at him. "I hope ye all enjoyed yer time whoring in Cornwall, but 'tis time to take our leave. As ye see, we have a guest on board. She is my guest and no man shall even look at her if he wishes to keep his eyes in his skull, ye ken?"

"Aye, Capt'n!" his crew responded.

"We sail for Scotland, lads! But first, we stop in London to deliver the lady to her betrothed in time for her wedding to the Queen's Vice-Admiral."

The men all booed and hissed, before returning to their duties. Relations between the Scottish and English had always been strained, but with the death of their Queen Mary and the English queen wishing to unite the two countries, tensions had run high and the men avoided English harbors whenever possible. They would fly the English flag and get Ruby as close as possible before securing her an escort, but Callum had no desire to step foot on English soil, nor to loiter in their waters longer than necessary. The queen tolerated piracy as long as it was in international waters and she profited, but Callum only shared with her when he needed favors, and none were needed on this day.

"Raise the anchor and hoist the sails! The *Devil of the Sea* is ready for adventure!" The men cheered and happily did his bidding, always ready to sail the high seas. Taking his place at the helm, Callum looked out to the horizon and took a deep breath of fresh air, the scent of brine a familiar companion. He needed to return home to his lands soon enough, but for now, the sea called to him like a siren beckoned a man to bed.

"May I take the helm?"

Speaking of sirens… Callum opened his eyes and looked down to see Ruby's golden curls blowing in the wind, blue eyes alight with excitement. Scanning her body, Callum frowned. "Ye are dressed as a lad."

"I found a pair of small breeches in that chest near your bed. Must belong to a child, but they fit me quite well, do they not?"

Ruby spun slowly, appearing as happy as a cat with a bowl of warm milk, but Callum bit his lower lip when he saw the curve of her arse nestled against the wool of the breeches and never had he envied a piece of fabric before. The tunic she wore was at least loose enough to hide the curve of her breasts, but for the love of all things holy, the lass had an arse made for all manner of sin.

"You do not approve? I simply felt it would be more comfortable while aboard the ship than dresses. I can put them back." Her face fell and she turned away, ready to walk back to the cabin.

Grabbing her arm, Callum pulled her back against him a wee bit harder than he meant to, and she fell into his arms with a breathless gasp. If he did not know for certain that she was a maiden, he would think her the most skilled temptress in all of England and Scotland combined. "It isnae that I dinnae approve, lass. 'Tis only that… well, they fit ye like a second skin. They were my wee cousin's, only he isnae so wee anymore, and I dare say they look better on ye than they ever did on him."

That made Ruby smile widely and Callum could not help but smile in return. Clearing his throat, he tried not to be affected by her cursed charms. The lass was going to put him under some spell if he did not keep his focus. "Ye will not wander the deck in those, ye ken. The men are not used to bonnie lassies aboard the ship, especially not ones wearing breeches. Ye must stick with me when ye leave the cabin. That is one rule I must force on ye."

Biting her lip, she nodded and looked over the rail, and Callum did the same. The sun was still low on the horizon but its rays shone upon the water's surface, making it glitter like a million fireflies. The beauty of the ocean never ceased to amaze him, yet the woman in front of him somehow astounded him with even more beauty than a summer sunset on the Atlantic Ocean.

Clearing his throat, Callum stepped aside and pointed to the helm. "Here. Take it."

"Really?" she asked with glee in her voice. "I grew up on ships, yet my papa never allowed me to help."

"I told ye. Ye get to make yer own decisions. Short of jumping overboard, I will deny ye nothing, my lady." Smiling widely, Ruby stepped up to the helm and took it in both her small hands, looking out to the ocean once more, the wind blowing in her golden hair.

When she started to veer them slightly off course, Callum moved behind her and placed his hands on top of hers, helping to get back on course. "Oh, I am sorry," she said with a laugh and he simply smiled, looking down at the top of her head, inhaling her sweet scent.

"'Tis quite all right, lass. Ye are doing just fine. I would just prefer to find London and not Spain," he said with a chuckle.

Sighing, she looked up at him with sadness in her eyes. "I would rather find Spain. I do not wish to go to London."

"Ye truly do not want to marry William, aye? He is a pompous arse, I ken. But he isnae so bad looking and will give ye a fine, kept living." The man was evil, but Callum bit his tongue, not wishing to poison her against a man she must live with for the rest of her life.

Taking her hands off the helm, Ruby quickly turned and looked up at him. With their faces only inches apart, he was reminded of their kiss and wished to kiss her once again, be damned the consequences, though he resisted. "I do not wish to be kept. What is it with everyone around me? Do I look like a spoiled woman who wishes to be catered to? I thought you understood me, Callum." Ducking under his arms, Ruby stormed down the set of stairs leading to the main deck, already breaking the one rule he had set for her.

Letting go of the helm, Callum commanded Samuel to take over as he followed Ruby down to the main deck, catching up with her in time to grab her arm and pull her to him. "Let go of me!" she demanded and tried to jerk out of his grip.

"I told ye. If ye want to be on deck, ye stay by me."

"Then do not insult me, and perhaps I shall."

"This is not up for debate, lass."

Walking toward his cabin, she opened the door and looked back at him. "Then I shall stay in here if it means I do not need to be near you." Ruby slammed the door – his door – and he blinked in disbelief. What had just happened?

Pushing the door open, Callum stepped in, confusion and irritation controlling every step. "I do understand ye, Ruby. Why else would I have offered to take ye to London?"

Pacing back and forth in his cabin, Ruby shook her head and placed her hands on her hips. Callum watched her hips sway with every step and she suddenly stopped, looking him in the eye. "There. That is why you brought me along."

"What is?" He frowned, crinkling his brow.

"I see how you look at me. This was all a ploy. You plan on bedding me."

Tilting his head back, Callum let out a laugh that made Ruby take a step back. The woman was out of her mind. "Dinnae flatter yerself, lass. Ye are bonnie, but so are many other women, and I can have one who is more experienced. I dinnae need to bed a maiden, nor do I wish to. I will get ye to your wedding and never think of ye a day in my life ever again. Ye can count on that."

Ruby narrowed her eyes at him and then just shrugged. "Good. Then we agree on that, at least."

"Indeed, we do." Callum inhaled and ran a hand through his hair, wondering why women had to be so damned complicated. "Now, I will return to the deck. If ye wish to join me, ye may now, otherwise, ye will be required to stay in here until the evening meal. What will it be?"

Plopping down on the bed, Ruby kicked off her boots and Callum looked at her wee perfect toes before she climbed into the bed. "I will stay here. I was up early hiding from my fate. I could use the rest, and some distance from you."

"Fine. As ye wish." Turning away, Callum shook his head and slammed the door harder than he meant to. But the lass ran hot and cold and he had no time for her tantrums. He had men to command and a ship to run. He did not regret offering to escort her, but he wondered if he had clearly thought through the situation. And, as much as it pained him, she was right about one thing. He had been in a cloud of lust when he decided to escort her. He was drawn to the lass, and her wild spirit only made him want to kiss her more.

Shouting a curse when he walked back to the deck, he saw his men staring at him with concern on their faces and he scowled, stomping up the stairs to the quarter deck where Samuel was at the helm. "Going well with the lass, aye?" Samuel raised a gray brow and smiled widely at Callum.

Looking askance at his first mate, Callum took the wheel and huffed out a frustrated breath. "I dinnae ken what I was thinking of bringing her along."

Scoffing, Samuel put his hands on his hips and shot Callum a knowing look with his gray eyes. "I ken exactly what ye were thinking."

"Aye, well. She is… different. Not like most lassies. And yet, she is just as fickle."

"Aye, ye say one wrong word, and the day is shot to shite," Samuel agreed. "But I never heard ye say a lass was *different*.

Perhaps ye have yer heart placed above yer cock for the first time in yer life."

Callum looked at Samuel and shook his head. "This is the last time I make that mistake ever again, I vow. I only meant to give her one last chance to experience the life she pines for, yet now I find myself facing sleeping on the floor of my own cabin."

"Ah, that's shite. Ye can sleep in my cabin, son," Samuel said, looking out at the ocean's horizon, covering his eyes against the bright sun.

"Oh, ye would give me yer bed, aye?"

Samuel smacked Callum on the back and snorted in amusement. "Och, I said ye can sleep in my cabin, not my bed."

"Why would I choose yer floor over mine, ye old goat?" Callum said, smiling at the man who was more like a father and trusted companion to him.

"Why? Because I ain't a bonnie lassie who is going to torture ye all night with unnecessary thoughts! Ye can fall asleep instead to the sounds of my snores, lad."

Callum smacked Samuel on the back and shook his head. "Ye are too kind. Now, keep steering. I have a ship to run." Walking away, Callum was tempted to go back to his cabin and check on Ruby, but he knew better than to interrupt an angry woman. Nay, his goal in life was to avoid storms. Not just the ones that would toss a man overboard, but also the ones that would bring a man to his knees.

He would leave the siren alone. He had promised to allow her freedom, and clearly, she wished to be away from him as much as he needed to be away from her.

Chapter 5

Staring up at the wooden planks on the ceiling, Ruby huffed with boredom and sat up in the bed when she heard a creak outside the door. Was Callum finally coming back? She had waited all cursed day for his return to apologize for her outburst. She knew he had taken great risks to help her escape being stuck on a ship with William. Instead, she was on a pirate ship with the most handsome man she had ever seen and he was giving her the opportunity of a lifetime. Rather than being grateful, she had stormed off in anger and he had left her here to rot.

What she truly wanted was another kiss. She still felt him on her, and being alone in his bed had been torture that she could no longer bear when every creak she heard failed to be his return. Hours had gone by and she grew restless, knowing she had to seek him out and apologize for her behavior.

Slipping her boots on, Ruby adjusted her breeches and tucked in her tunic before heading out the door. The sun that had blinded her earlier had been replaced by dull blue moonlight that subtly lit the otherwise dark void of the night. Stepping onto the deck, Ruby saw no men and frowned. Her first day aboard the ship had been spent in solitude and it was all her own fault.

"Callum?" she called softly as she walked up to the quarter-deck, but nobody was there. Voices and laughter drifted to her on the wind and she strained to locate its origin. Remembering her time aboard ships with her papa, she knew immediately where to find the men.

Descending the stairs down to the crew's quarters, the voices became louder and she heard singing and the very poor playing of what sounded like rudimentary instruments. A wide smile spread across her face as she remembered hearing similar songs sung by her papa's men aboard his ship while they were working on the deck, keeping pace with the rhythm of their words.

When she reached the sleeping quarters, Ruby saw the men clapping their hands while one man played the flute and another banged what looked like a stick against a tin can. Ruby laughed to herself but appreciated their will to make merry with what little resources they had. This was the pirate life she longed to live. The fulfillment of a hard day's work, a less than appetizing meal, yet knowing a new adventure lay ahead on the next day... and perhaps a merchant ship loaded with food and coins to be had.

The itch to join the men in their fun had Ruby tapping her toes along with the rhythm of the tin can, but she remembered Callum's warning to stay close to him. Looking around the room lit by lanterns attached to the walls, she saw no sign of the captain, so she began to back up slowly and head back to his cabin. She had no idea where he could be, but he was not here. A man like Callum did not blend into a crowd.

"Oy! 'Tis that English lass the captain brought on board!" one man shouted and the music stopped as the room went silent. Cursing under her breath, Ruby plastered a smile on her face and turned to look at the crowd of bedraggled men who all stared back at her with some sort of anticipation.

"Uh... hello." She wiggled her fingers instead of a wave, not certain what she was to do or say.

"Ye looking to join the fun, aye?" a man with a thick Scottish brogue asked, and Ruby looked around the room once more.

"I... uh... was looking for Callum, er... Lord Argyll."

"Och, we just call him Capt'n here!" One man laughed and the rest followed suit. "He isnae here, lass. But ye are, and ye should have yerself some fun, aye?"

"Aye!" the men said and one stepped forward and removed his hat, bowing as regally as any nobleman she had ever known, but when he looked back at her, his toothless grin made her smile. The delight in his eyes was contagious, so when he put out his hand, Ruby laughed and took it, allowing him to drag her into the middle of the room. The music started up once more and the men began to whoop and clap their hands when the old pirate who held her hand began to dance like a fool.

Tilting her head back to laugh, Ruby kicked off her boots and started to move her bare feet, dancing as she used to years ago on her papa's ship. The men clapped and hollered as she took the center of the room, kicking her feet up and spinning around, feeling her hair whirl around behind her. One man shoved a mug of ale into her hand and she took it gladly, stopping just long enough to gulp it down in one breath before putting it out for more. A man with a reddish-orange beard tilted his mug against hers, giving Ruby the rest of his drink and she nodded in thanks, drinking it down and wiping the froth from her upper lip before going back to her dance.

Ruby wasn't certain if the room spun because of the ale or her feet, but it did not matter. She was having more fun than she could ever remember and the men laughed and sang, encouraging her to continue. But when a growl filled the room and the music abruptly stopped, Ruby looked over her shoulder just in time to see Callum storming toward her, shirtless with wet hair dripping on his shoulders, perhaps from having just bathed, eyes ablaze with rage.

He reached out and grabbed her arm, dragging her toward him before she could even steady herself. As her body crashed into his, she gasped and struggled, hearing the men in the background whispering to each other before speaking out. "Och, come now, Capt'n! She was just having a wee bit of fun!"

"Aye! Let the lass stay!"

Callum looked at her, his olive eyes boring into hers with some unspoken warning before he hoisted her over his shoulder like a sack of grain, her head dangling near his backside. "I will deal with ye men on the morrow!" Callum shouted as he stormed out of the sleeping quarters with Ruby pummeling his bare, sculpted back with her fists and yelling curses she was certain he heard, yet ignored.

"Put me down, you bastard, curse you!" she yelled, smacking his arse with her hand and realizing it was as hard as stone when her palms began to sting. "You are a brute!"

"And ye are a poor listener!" he shouted, stomping up the stairs, onto the deck and over to his cabin door. With one hard kick, the door swung inward and he deftly lifted her off his shoulder, tossing her onto the bed.

"I listen just fine! I was alone for hours!" Trying to jump off the bed, Ruby grunted with frustration when he pushed her back down onto his mattress and bore down on her. His dark hair hung around his face and only then did she notice the muscular ridges of his chest covered with a light dusting of dark hair. Breath quickening, she was suddenly acutely aware that Callum was pressing his weight down onto her, pinning her arms over her head.

"I was looking for you," she whispered, having no more desire to shout.

"It did not appear that way. Ye were looking for the attention of every other man aboard this ship. That is how it appeared," he said gruffly.

Widening her eyes, Ruby looked at his chest, so close to hers, then back to his eyes. "That is not at all true. I was simply enjoying the music as I did when I was a young girl aboard my papa's ship. You sound jealous," she added breathlessly, knowing he was not, but wishing he was for some unknown reason.

"Jealousy is not an emotion I am capable of feeling, lass."

"What are you capable of feeling?" she asked, truly wanting to learn more about this hard man. He was a gentle-born man, yes, yet no gentleman pirate. Had he ever loved a woman? Had a close family? Friends?

"Lust. I feel lust." When he abruptly pushed off her, she felt her insides flutter and her heart leap as he stood up straight and walked away. His chest glowed in the dim lantern light and the shadows on his face made him look ominous and dangerous. With his breeches hanging low on his hips, she could see the muscles that narrowed down below his waist, a small trail of dark hairs leading to the part of him she had felt only the night before as she sat on his lap.

"Lust... for me?" His change in mood confused her. He went from angry to defeated in the blink of an eye.

"Aye, for ye!" Turning mid-step, Callum ran a hand through his hair and growled. "What is it about ye, lass? Thoughts of ye have consumed my mind since yesterday when I arrived. Are ye a witch? The fae? Have ye put a spell on me? I cannae decide whether to shake ye or kiss ye at any given moment!"

Sitting up on the bed, Ruby smoothed her hair and tapped the mattress with her fingers as she observed the man pacing across the room. How could a man so strong, handsome, and feral believe himself bewitched by a woman? If anything, he was the one who had put a spell on her. She had not stopped thinking of him, or that kiss, or the feel of his hands on her for a single second since the night before. They had only met a day ago and yet she was so drawn to him like their souls were woven from the same cut of cloth. Though he angered her earlier, she knew he understood her and had risked much to deliver her to London.

Standing up slowly, Ruby walked over to him and touched his arm from behind. He spun around and looked down at her. "Kiss me."

"What?" he asked, shaking his head and narrowing his eyes.

"You said you do not know whether to shake me or kiss me. I am telling you that you should kiss me."

Scoffing, Callum turned away and stared at the shelf on the wall where he kept his charts, maps, and pistol at the ready. "That is the last thing I should do, lass."

"I disagree," she said, standing her ground and coming up behind him once more, wanting more than anything to feel his lips on hers once more.

"Dinnae make this harder than it needs to be. Ye are on yer way to London to marry the Vice-Admiral. Ye would do well to remember that."

This time, Ruby scoffed and turned away. "Remember? I remember every second of every day. I have only a few days left before I must marry a man I do not like, let alone love. There is something about him I do not trust."

"Ye shouldnae trust him, Ruby. He is not worthy of it."

"What does that mean?" Turning back toward him, she noticed he was still facing the wall, but she refused to be avoided. "Callum, look at me."

Turning slowly, he did as she asked, but the look of disgust on his face made her shrink back. "You know something about him, don't you?" Ruby questioned. "Tell me."

"It is not my place to tell ye anything. Ye must marry him, regardless of what I ken. But, aye. I have had... business with him in the past."

"Business?" Ruby pursed her lips and cocked her head in confusion. What sort of business would a Scottish pirate have with an English Vice-Admiral?

"Ye need to get some sleep. We have an early morning and I cannae trust ye to stay put if left alone." Callum kicked off his boots and sat on the edge of the bed.

"Wha- what are you doing?" Ruby asked, crossing her arms.

"I am getting into my bed. What are ye doing?" Callum replied, laying down and pulling the sheet over his body.

"Where am I to sleep?"

"I dinnae ken, but ye should have thought of that before ye broke the one rule I gave ye... again. I cannae have ye dancing in breeches around my drunken men."

"I am used to dealing with the crew. I grew up on a ship, lest you forget."

Sitting up in the bed, Callum looked at her and narrowed his green eyes. "Ye arenae used to *my* men and *they* arenae used to bonnie lassies dancing in breeches." Rolling away from her, Callum faced the wall and closed his eyes.

Ruby huffed in frustration and rolled her eyes. He called her bonnie, yet he refused to kiss her again. She did not care if she was on her way to London to be married. She was not married yet, and as far as she was concerned her freedom did not end until that day, and even after, she would fight for every ounce of independence she could get.

If Callum wanted to be stubborn, she could be even more so. There was no way she was sleeping on the floor. Callum appeared to already be asleep, his breathing rhythmic as his back rose and fell with subtle motion. Ruby undid her borrowed breeches and slipped into the other side of the bed as carefully as possible, not wanting to wake the man up. She had had enough arguing for the day and simply wished to sleep. In truth, she wished for much more than that, but for now, sleep was better than staring at the wall or ceiling for another few hours. Untying the string on the top of her tunic, Ruby laid down and rolled away from Callum so their backs faced one another.

He was a frustrating man, for certain. Yet, she could not get the memory of his touch out of her head, nor the feel of him. Being so close to him made her body tingle with sensations she wished to avoid. She wished to avoid Callum altogether at this point, but as long as they both stayed in this position throughout the night, she could at least awaken early and sneak out of the bed before he ever even knew she was there.

Something warm and soft nestled against his thighs and his hand rested on something else entirely. Moving his other hand slowly downward, he felt the unmistakable curves and smooth skin of a woman's backside pressed against his groin. Opening his eyes with a start, Callum saw blonde curls spread across the pillow before him and the sleek bare shoulder of a small woman. Lifting his head to look over her body, Callum groaned when reality crashed down on him. Not only was Ruby Berry pressed dangerously close to his body, but her tunic had slipped down during the night and his arm was wrapped beneath her body, his hand cradling one of her exposed breasts. Her pink, erect nipples stood proudly for his gazing pleasure and he felt himself immediately grow hard, thankful he was still wearing his breeches, even if they were hanging low on his hips.

Realizing his other hand rested on her bare hip, Callum froze and laid his head back on the pillow, wondering how he ended up in such a position, and more importantly, how he was going to get out of it… not that he wanted to. He would much rather roll over on top of her, spread her legs and bury his face between her thighs. By the devil, the woman was not even wearing breeches. It would be so simple… and yet his life would become so much more complicated. She was not his to possess and yet somehow, he knew that being with Ruby would be a life-altering experience, one that would change his very existence. And, not just because her father would kill him.

When she began to stir, Callum attempted to pull his arm from beneath her, but that only made her eyes flutter awake. Her blue irises focused on his face when she looked over her shoulder. "Callum?"

"Aye." His voice was raspy and not with sleep. She was disheveled with rosy cheeks and sweeping lashes, her hair messed up from the night, and yet she looked more beautiful than ever, and it had nothing to do with her lovely breasts still rising and falling before his eyes with her every breath.

When she began to become aware of her surroundings, Ruby looked down and noticed her exposed breasts, his arm trapped beneath her, and his hand still grazing her nipple. "Oh, my," she breathed, but she did not try to move away.

"I—" For the first time in as long as he could remember, Callum was at a loss for words. "I woke up like… this." He wiggled his fingers to try to emphasize his point, but when he brushed against her nipple again, she inhaled sharply and stared him in the eye.

"Oh. And your other hand is…"

Callum moved his free hand off her backside where he forgot he had left it while trying to move his trapped hand. Ruby arched and rolled onto her back to help free his arm, but all that did was bring her breasts closer to his face. His hand tingled from lack of circulation and his cock strained from far too much circulation. By the devil, was she trying to seduce him? It was bloody working.

Ruby slowly pulled her tunic back up her shoulders and covered her breasts, much to Callum's simultaneous disappointment and relief. "Ye came into the bed I see."

"Yes. After you fell asleep. I do not think I had many choices. However, I did not expect to awaken like that."

"Nor I," he grumbled, running his hands through his hair and feeling more tension in his loins than he ever had in his life. She was this untouchable woman, yet he had touched her once. It had been no more than a kiss, yet it had been more powerful than any encounter he had ever had with a woman in his life. "I had intended on sleeping in my first mate's quarters until I found ye dancing in the middle of all my men."

Ruby rolled her eyes and turned toward him. "Do not start on that again, Callum. I already explained it to you, and you said I could make my own decisions. I decided to dance." She shrugged and he noticed her gaze roam down his chest before returning to his eyes again.

Nodding, Callum looked at her. "Ye are right, lass. I did make ye that promise. And I left ye in here alone all day. I apologize."

"I chose to stay in here all day, Callum. But today…" Ruby sat up in the bed and moved toward the edge with her back facing him, stretching her arms up high in the air. "I choose to stay on deck. I vow to stay by your side… if you do not tire of my company."

When Ruby got out of the bed, Callum caught a peek of her lovely round, bare arse just before she turned away and wrapped a sheet around her body. Dear God, he was going to die if all the blood kept rushing downward. "I willnae tire of ye, lass." He did his best to sound unaffected. He was certain she did not intend for him to see her breasts or her arse and did not wish to embarrass her, but never had he fought so fiercely against taking a woman in his arms. She was an unusual woman. Still a maiden, yet so bloody sensual, Ruby did not seem unnerved by having awoken with his hand on her breast. She had chosen to share his bed yet waited for him to fall asleep before doing so. She was not attempting to seduce him, he decided, but that made her allure even more potent. She was not the sort of woman he was used to. She had goals, dreams, intelligence, beauty, wit, and with a fire running through her veins, and he was the moth attracted to her flame.

"We shall see about that," she giggled, running her fingers through her messy curls. "I can be a bit much; I am aware of it."

Climbing out of the bed, Callum bent over and picked up his tunic, slipping it over his head and feeling her burning gaze on him. The tension in the room was thicker than the fog on a freezing Atlantic morning in winter, and he felt the pulse of desire flowing between him and Ruby. They could both act unaffected by the events of the morning, but their relationship had shifted beyond casual, if it could ever have been considered as much. From the moment he set eyes on her, he felt his world shift, but now, he was permanently off-kilter every time she came near.

"Then, we shall see." Callum tightened his breeches, tied his hair back into a queue, and slipped on his boots. "I will leave ye to get dressed. My men will be waiting for me." Suddenly feeling the need to flee before he took her in his arms and delivered on the kiss she had asked for the night before, Callum cleared his throat and stepped out of the cabin.

The sun was just creeping over the horizon to the east and he inhaled, ready to take on a new day on the water, smelling adventure in the air and feeling a tightening in his chest… or maybe he was just feeling a cursed clenching in his heart. What had she done to him? More women than he could even count or remember had shared his bed, and yet, this one woman had consumed his thoughts in just the two days that he had known her.

Since the day his father was killed in a pirate hunt led by that bastard Stanhope, Callum had remained closed to the world of the living. He had inherited his father's titles and lands, but loyalty to a church or any individual got a man nowhere in this changing world. One day Scotland prevailed, the next day England. One day Catholics ruled, the next day Protestants. From a young age, Callum understood that the only loyalty that was required was to himself and his men, who not only depended on him but also aided him in his desire to avoid the stale existence of a noble-born Scottsman in an unstable world. Here on the rocking ocean waves, he was just a man living in the moment, there one day and gone the next, never having attachments beyond the rails of his ship. Then Ruby Berry appeared in his life and he knew that as always, she would be no more than a whisper on the wind, a face from his past that he would likely forget soon enough.

But for now, her face was all he saw. The rays of the sun glittered gold like the fine-spun strands of her hair. It's blazing reflection sparkled red, like the plump flesh of her lips, and the sea could never be as blue as her eyes. Shaking his head and cursing himself a fool, Callum stomped up to the helm and shouted at his men, already hard at work.

"We should reach our destination by the morrow, men!" The crew shouted, knowing that any trip between Cornwall and London would be an easy enough one if the weather did not fight back, and always happy to find a harbor town where ale and women could be found. "We have one more night aboard the ship before we deliver Miss Berry and I expect ye all to be on yer best behavior with the lass, unlike last night."

The crew went silent, not certain if a punishment was awaiting them and in truth, he should force more hours of labor on them for the night, perhaps make them scrub the decks or empty the chamber pots all night rather than eat. Yet, he knew firsthand how enchanting the lass was. She commanded a room full of men, had them eating out of the palm of her hand. He felt the same way and decided he should not punish them for being enchanted by an enchantress.

"So, I expect ye all to work hard, for tomorrow we shall celebrate another safe journey before heading home."

"Scotland!" one man yelled and Callum smiled.

"Aye! The land of Scots, whiskey, bonnie lassies, and haggis!" His men laughed and went back to their duties while he turned back to the sea, slightly saddened to realize his time with Ruby was so short-lived and coming to an end, yet knowing it was for the best. Whatever he was feeling for the woman was nothing more than infatuation and as soon as she was out of his sight, he could continue his life and surely forget about her existence. How hard could it be to forget a woman he has only known for three days?

Chapter 6

Excited for another day aboard Callum's ship, Ruby finished lacing up the bodice of her burgundy dress and slipped on her leather shoes, ready to join him on deck. Though she had enjoyed wearing breeches, Ruby had decided to don her dresses once more. Callum had seemed rather unhappy about her clothing choice the day before and even more upset about her being around his men. She could not understand why he cared so much but decided to call a truce and wear a comfortable dress.

Walking out into the sun, another glorious spring day awaited her, and Ruby took a deep breath, knowing her days of freedom drew to an end with every hour that passed. She was not certain when they would reach London, but enough time aboard ship as a child had taught her that her home was not very far from London.

Spotting Callum speaking with Samuel, she smiled and felt the sun warm her face while anticipation warmed the rest of her body with each step bringing her closer to him. He was a Scot and though most English were bred to consider them primitive and violent, Ruby knew better. They were a proud, repressed people who fought for what they believed in and preferred death over being controlled by a monarch they did not call their own. Though there was more to Callum than she understood, it was a story he kept buried deep within. She longed to know his truths yet feared she never would.

When he saw her approaching, there was a look in his eyes and he raised his brow. Appreciation was written in his features but she was not certain if it was because of her decision to wear a dress or how she looked in it. Though she hoped for the latter, it was only the night before that he had rejected her. Although, something had changed between them this morning. He had seen her nearly undressed and he did not seem displeased. And though she knew that a maiden should feel ashamed, she felt only excitement, which proved to her that she was more wicked and wanton than perhaps she should be. Yet, it had been an accident, a situation that arose unexpectedly, and feeling his hands on her, even if by mistake, had made her tingle all over, as did the feel of his hard rod pressed against her backside. And the look in his eyes told her he was remembering those moments, as well.

"Good morning," she said with a smile to Samuel, who tipped his hat and took her hand up to his mouth for a quick kiss.

"Mornin' to ye, Miss Berry. 'Tis a lovely day, is it not? But my keen nose smells a storm brewing. Make no mistake, we will feel the sea's wrath by nightfall."

Ruby nodded and took a deep breath, having sensed the same, yet too focused on Callum to have truly recognized it until just now.

"I believe you are correct," she said, looking at Callum who now intently looked out to the horizon. Though he played at studying the weather, Ruby felt he was intentionally avoiding her. Most women would pine for a man's attentions, but Ruby knew better than that. She had no need to, for she was to marry another man. But for now, she understood that the man wanted what he could not have. Deciding to avoid him as well, Ruby turned away and stepped up to Samuel, linking arms with him and smiling up at his mature yet handsome face. "What else do you sense, Mister Smith?"

Samuel gave her a wide grin and wrapped an arm around her shoulders in a fatherly embrace. "I sense an opportunity, ye ken."

Looking up at him quizzically, Ruby shook her head in confusion. "I am sorry, but I do not 'ken'," she replied, enjoying the sound of the Scottish word on her tongue. "An opportunity for what?"

"For riches, perhaps. Freedom for ye…" leaning in, Samuel whispered into her ear. "And mayhap even love." He waggled his brows and she frowned, not understanding. He gestured over his shoulder with a nod of his head, and she followed his cue, seeing Callum standing close by intentionally ignoring them.

"Oh, well. That is impossible. You know I am to be married once we reach London."

Making a tsking sound, Samuel guided her over to the rail of the ship and they stared down at the water splashing against the hull. "I dinnae ken what ye marrying that Englishman has to do with loving Callum, or him loving ye."

Feeling her face flush, Ruby cleared her throat. "Oh, no. You have it all wrong, Mister Smith. I am here because Callum invited me to have a few days of freedom before I marry William. He felt for my plight, and that was all."

"Whatever ye say, Miss. I can tell ye that I have kenned him his entire life. I was his father's first mate before his. He has never invited a woman to sail with us. Make of that what ye will."

Ruby pursed her lips and nodded, not at all sure she agreed with his version of events. It was clear Callum was attracted to her. But what he spoke of—love—was something else entirely. She and Callum shared an adventurous spirit and a love of the sea, but that was all. There was no love between them and she was quite sure he could not wait to be rid of her.

"Mister Smith, when will we reach the harbor of London?"

"Oh, Capt'n believes we shall arrive by tomorrow night. From there, we will secure ye a carriage to take ye to yer man."

Tomorrow? Her heart squeezed painfully in her chest. This journey had only just begun and already it was at an end. And, though Callum may be glad to be rid of her, she felt a keen pain at the thought of never seeing him again, never knowing his mysteries, or feeling his kiss again. Looking over her shoulder, Ruby caught Callum watching her and Samuel, but he quickly looked away and scowled once more. No, he did not love her. The man did not even like her. She was a burden, stuck by his side until they reached their destination.

Sighing, Ruby looked at Samuel and leaned in. "I assume you can manage the ship for a few moments without Callum? I have a few things I would like to discuss with him in private, if I may."

Raising a brow, Samuel grinned at her. "Of course I can, Miss. I think ye and the Capt'n have much to sort out, indeed."

She was not at all certain what Samuel believed she planned to discuss with Callum that would require such a reaction, but in the end, it was not his business. Ruby only had one day left with Callum, the man who had risked much simply to allow her some freedom for a few days, and not only did she wish to thank him, she had some questions for him that needed answering before she disembarked from the ship.

Walking over to Callum, who stared determinedly out to sea, Ruby stepped in front of him to snap him out of whatever deep thoughts had him in such a daze. "Callum?"

"Aye?" he replied but did not break his concentration or look at her. It was as if he looked through her, as if she was naught more than an insect buzzing around his head that he wished to swat away. Well, damn it all, he had invited her onto this ship and seemed determined to keep her near, yet at arm's length all the cursed time, and the tension between them was becoming more than she could bear.

"I wish to speak with you."

"Speak, then."

"In private, if you please."

"And if I dinnae please?"

Putting her hands on her hips, Ruby got on her tiptoes, trying fruitlessly to reach his eye level. "We can discuss our... situation this morning in front of your crew, if you prefer."

"'Tis not as if they havenae kenned me to awaken with a lassie's breasts in my hands." He shrugged and finally looked down at her, flashing a smug grin. Was he trying to anger her? Perhaps make her jealous? Oddly, it was working, and that only raised her hackles more.

"Curse you, Callum! Will you speak with me or not?" Ruby stomped her foot in frustration and stormed down the steps onto the main deck, toward his cabin without looking back. She did not even care if he followed her or not. He had offered to take her to London, had promised her the right to make her own choices during the journey, yet he constantly went to war with everything she asked for.

Opening the cabin door, Ruby stepped in and tried to shut it behind her, but Callum stuck his booted foot through just in time. When he stepped in and shut the door, turning to look at her with his large arms crossed over his chest as if he was irritated for having been interrupted, she rolled her eyes and turned away.

"Well, I'm here. What did ye wish to say, lass?"

"I had wished to thank you for offering to take me, you lout! I am trying to get along with you, but every time I think I can, you grow sour once more and treat me like I am no more than a stowaway! But make no mistake, I am here because you suggested I disappear until William's ship was gone! Yet nothing I do or say can satisfy you, and so far every decision I have tried to make has been rejected!"

Stepping closer with his arms still crossed, Callum looked down at her with narrowed eyes. "Ye mean yer decision to wear breeches that form to yer arse like a second skin, dancing and drinking ale with my men? Or yer decision to ask fer another kiss from me as we sail toward yer betrothed? I apologize if I am only trying to save ye from making mistakes and having regrets." His tone of voice was cold and somehow, without even having raised his voice, he had properly scolded her much as her father would have.

"I have been coddled and protected for years, forced to wear painfully heavy dresses with tight bodices that restrict my breathing, never allowed to decide anything for myself! I used to be allowed on the ships, but after my cousin died on her father's ship, my father grew worried and protective, doing all he could to keep me away from the family business and tucked away indoors! 'Tis why he betrothed me to William, who vowed to keep me as a little wife who does naught but bear his children and mend his clothing while he sails the seas and has freedoms of his own!"

"'Tis the way of the world and has been for centuries. Ye cannae expect much more." His casual shrug as if her feelings, desires, and dreams no longer mattered, was enough to drain the fight from her.

"Why do you hate me?" Ruby whispered as his words cut her like a million shards of broken glass. "I know you do not believe that. You would not have brought me here if you did. You said you understood me. Now you wish to simply treat me the same way every other man does. What have I done to make you treat me so cruelly?"

Callum growled and spun away from her, pacing the floor of his cabin for a few seconds before facing her again. "What have ye done? Ye really want to ken the answer to that, Ruby?"

"Yes! I do! What have I done to earn your perpetual scorn, Callum Campbell?"

Striding over to her, Callum grabbed Ruby's waist and pulled her against his body, making her gasp when his lips crashed down on hers almost painfully, like he was a man dying of thirst and she was the only oasis in a vast desert. She wanted to melt into his arms, wrap herself around him, and feel his lips on hers all night long. Instead, she pushed him away.

"What are you doing?" she whispered, quivering so fiercely she feared her knees would give out and she would fall to the ground like a ridiculous woman.

"I am kissing ye, just as ye asked!" he shouted, and she pulled away even more, feeling anger, resentment, and some unknown emotion building inside of her gut. It felt like need, the need for acceptance, like longing for companionship and love… but not from any man. She wanted all of it from this man who only kissed her because she asked, not because he wished to.

In the end, he was naught more than a womanizing pirate, incapable of genuine care for another.

"So, that is it then? You are angry at me for asking you to kiss me? Well, I apologize, Lord Argyll, for offending you with my ill manners. I vow never to put you in such a position again. I did not believe you were a man of such morality. By the morrow, I will no longer cause you problems."

Ruby turned up her nose and spun on her heel, marching toward the door, determined to be away from Callum before he witnessed her weakness as tears began to flood her eyes.

Before she could make it to the door, she felt herself being dragged back by the arm once more and quickly turned around to scold him. "Callum!" she cried. "Just leave me alone! You have made yourself perfectly clear!"

His large hands wrapped around her waist as he slowly guided her backward until she felt the wooden wall pressed against her back.

"Have I? I dinnae think I have, lass." His forehead pressed against hers, and she looked up into his light green eyes, her heart beating wildly as she tried to catch her breath. His tanned skin was a contrast to her alabaster English tone, but it only stood as a testament to the lifestyle he lived upon a ship, with the warmth of the sun shining down on him all day. It was exciting, yet it saddened her to know she would never share that life.

"Then what is your point, Lord Argyll?" she whispered, feeling his breath fanning her face as hers escaped in short pants.

"Ye have caused me a problem, indeed. A verra big problem. That is my point."

Ruby struggled to break away, wishing to kick him in the shin. Must he always insult her very existence? "Then do leave me be! And I will cease to cause you trouble." More tears rolled down her cheeks, and she hurried to wipe them away, but it was futile. More continued to flow until she could hardly see. Curse this man. If he hated her so much, why would he not just let her go?

Shaking his head, Callum narrowed his eyes and bit his bottom lip in a way that made Ruby tingle from toe to scalp. "The problem is that I cannae stop thinking of ye, Ruby!" he nearly shouted, and Ruby crinkled her brow with confusion. "Curse the devil, ye have consumed my thoughts!"

"I… I did not mean to…" she stuttered, shaking her head slowly and looking at him carefully, feeling something tug at her heart. It could not be joy, for there was no hope for them. She would be gone from him on the morrow and William's wife a few days after that. But to know he reciprocated her feelings made her stomach flutter as if a hundred butterflies took flight simultaneously.

"I ken ye didnae. That is what makes ye even more exasperating!"

"Well… well.." She stumbled on her words, trying to find a way to express how she felt about him, as well. He thought she was exasperating? He was the most complicated man she had ever known. Why would he yell at her for his feelings? "I feel the same way!" she shouted at him, pushing against his chest and feeling the hard ridges of muscle beneath her palms, which only reminded her of how he looked without his tunic on. Her cheeks grew hot and she knew she was blushing. Curse her fair skin for betraying her every emotion!

"You feel the same? That ye think I am exasperating? Or that ye cannae stop thinking of me?" he persisted, locking his eyes on hers, awaiting an answer.

"Yes."

"To which one?"

"Y-yes," she responded, knowing she was being stubborn. Why was it so hard to say how she felt? Yes, she was due to marry another man, but was she not allowed to have her own thoughts, emotions, and the right to express them?

"Devil's bollocks, Ruby! Yes to what?" he shouted.

"All of it, curse you! I have only known you for three days and yet it feels like three years! How can that be? I am honestly asking because it makes no sense to me! Yes, you are exasperating! The most frustrating man I have ever known! And yes, I cannot stop thinking of you for even a moment! I want to be near you, then I wish to run away!"

"What do ye want, Ruby?" he asked with a sudden softness, running a finger over her cheek so gently that her eyes closed and a sigh left her parted lips. "Tell me."

"You," she whispered. "I want you, Callum Campbell."

"Ye already have me, lass." Leaning in, Callum touched his lips to hers, gentle at first but as she pressed herself closer to him, he seemed to lose all control of himself, deepening the kiss, slipping his tongue inside her mouth. She groaned, loving the feel of his tongue on hers once again. It was the single most sensual feeling she had ever had, the way they melded together, a fever burning between them.

His hands rested on her hips and she wrapped hers around his neck, pulling him even closer. She could feel every inch of him pressed against every inch of her, feel the hard length of his manhood pressing against her belly. She remembered how it had felt against her bare skin only a few hours ago, remembered the feel of his calloused palm resting on her breast. How she longed to relive those moments with him.

When his hand started slowly exploring the rest of her body, inching hesitantly toward her breasts, she felt an ache deep within that she had never felt more strongly in all her life. Her nipples grew harder and sensitive, straining to be in his palms once more. Ruby pressed against him, trying to communicate without words that she wanted his touch, needed it.

He moaned and pushed himself into her, trapping Ruby even tighter between him and the wall. Deftly, his fingers tugged at the laces of her bodice and she felt the linen fabric grow slack as he continued to devour her mouth, his tongue dancing with hers, mimicking all the wanton things he wished to do with her body.

"Good God, Ruby," he murmured when his mouth traveled down to her throat and his hands slid her dress and shift down her shoulders at the same time. "Ye are so beautiful. And ye taste so good." Never had she heard a man tell her that she tasted good, and something about those words made her want so much more. Tilting her head back, Ruby gave him better access to her neck, shivering when his tongue slid down its length as his hands cupped her exposed breasts.

When his thumbs ran across the hard tips of her nipples, Ruby groaned and instinctively arched her back into his touch. "Ye like that, do ye?" he asked, his mouth now kissing her collarbone, his hot breath trailing over her flesh. "Tell me, Ruby."

"Yes! God, yes..." Ruby sighed, then gasped when his warm tongue flicked over her nipple, and she looked down, feeling another intense wave of desire wash over her when she saw him gently taking her breast into his mouth. "Oh, my," she groaned.

"Ye are..." Callum slid his tongue across her breast and over to the other, giving it the same loving attention. "Absolute perfection," he whispered before latching onto the other breast and sucking it until her knees felt weak and her hands were pulling at his dark hair.

"Callum..."

He murmured a reply but she could not understand his words when he was still fondling her nipple with his tongue. Sliding his tongue back up her neck, Callum took her lips once more in a kiss so full of need that Ruby felt as if she may swoon. She was not at all certain how far this was going or what Callum intended, but she was certain she would allow him to do absolutely anything he wished, even take her maidenhead, and damn the consequences. She may regret it one day, but right now, her body craved to be touched by him.

Her dress hung slack around her hips. She was half-naked and in his arms, but it wasn't enough. She needed more contact. Removing her dress, she felt it slide down her legs before pooling around her ankles on the ground. Callum pulled away, but only enough to observe her completely naked body and she shivered, hoping her first time completely undressed in front of a man did not end up in humiliation. She knew Callum had been with other women, perhaps dozens. She did not know how she compared, but right now she felt beautiful. Callum made her feel confident, like a real woman who could say what she wanted and be herself.

"My God." Callum ran his warm hands down her back, across her hips, and over to her backside where his fingers carefully grazed her skin, making her break out in gooseflesh. When she shivered, Callum looked at her with wonder in his eyes. "Ye are the most beautiful woman I have ever kenned, Ruby Berry."

She shook her head with disbelief. "Now I know you lie," she replied. "That cannot be true."

"I never lie, lass. I wouldnae say such a thing, if it werenae the truth. Nor have I ever uttered those words to another woman. You are a masterpiece, love."

Love? She swallowed hard, deciding not to allow his words to be misunderstood. Surely he did not mean it in such a way. "I want to see you, Callum. All of you."

Leaning in, he kissed her so softly that her heart melted. His hands roamed her body and when they rested just below her navel, she slightly flexed her hips, hoping he would touch her where she ached the most.

"Are ye certain?" he asked with sincerity and she nodded. She wanted to see every last inch of his sculpted body.

"I am." Taking a deep breath and mustering her courage, Ruby ran a finger over the bulge in his breeches and Callum groaned, tearing his tunic off and throwing it onto the floor. His perfectly chiseled torso was a sight to behold and Ruby ran her hands over every ridge, feeling the coarse hairs tickle her fingertips. That same trail of hair she had noticed before felt rough to the touch, and Callum stood still and watched as Ruby explored, stopping at the top of his breeches.

He groaned when she gently ran her finger over the front of his breeches once more and slowly unbuttoned them. When they slackened on his hips, she watched as he pushed them down, gasping when his erect manhood sprang free, pointed directly at her. "Oh, my," she whispered, reaching out to touch it and then pulling back immediately. It was somehow rock hard yet smooth to the touch at the same time. "I am… new to this," she confessed, feeling slightly embarrassed.

"I ken, lass. We won't do anything ye do not wish to do."

"What if I want to do all of it?" she asked, raising a brow and his eyes widened.

"Ye cannae mean—"

"Everything, Callum."

"I cannae." He shook his head and frowned. "Ruby, we cannae."

"Yes, we can. It appears you are most capable," she said, touching his hard length once more, this time wrapping her hand around it, watching in wonder as his eyes drooped to half-mast when he watched her grip him.

"That is not what I mean." His voice was strained and she could tell he was using all his effort to hold back. Releasing her grip, Ruby frowned and bent over to pull her dress up, disappointment flooding her. She understood why Callum resisted her desires, but rejection overwhelmed her.

"Nay. Not yet," Callum growled and before she could prepare herself, she felt him swoop her up behind the knees as he carried her in his arms. "I dinnae want that dress back on ye just yet."

Before she could ask questions, Callum tossed her onto the bed, her naked body laid out before him. "I willnae take yer maidenhead, Ruby. It would be wrong. I ken ye are upset but ye must trust me. Someday ye will thank me. But that doesnae mean I cannae pleasure ye, love."

"Oh?" Ruby had no idea what he was talking about. They were both completely naked and somehow she felt so comfortable in front of him like she was safe and treasured.

"Oh, aye. May I show ye?" He stood before her, his erection jutting out proudly and all she could do was nod her head, having no idea what he planned to do, but trusting him with her body.

Callum crawled onto the bed and propped himself up on his elbows as he hovered over her, kissing her passionately for several torturous moments as his hands roamed over her body, caressing her breasts, hips, and backside, even her inner thighs without touching her where she truly ached to feel him.

"Please," she asked with frustration when his finger, once again, grazed her inner thigh so close to her center, then pulled away.

"Please what, love?" he asked, kissing down her neck, stopping at her breasts to suck on each nipple until they became hard peaks once more. "Is this what ye want?" His finger finally touched her core and she gasped, arching her back and spreading her legs slightly when he nipped at her breast with his teeth and stroked the place between her legs that sent a shock of pure pleasure throughout her entire body.

"Yes!" she shouted both in frustration and ecstasy.

"Well why didnae ye just tell me?" he said with a grin that made her want to slap and kiss him at the same time. But then his head moved back down her body, this time stopping at her navel while his finger weaved some form of magic, working in circles over that one spot that drove her mad. His lips kissed her pelvis bone and a finger slipped inside her while his other continued its skilled ministrations. Something so powerful, so intense, washed over her, causing her to nearly lift off the bed as she bit her lip to keep from screaming out in pleasure. "Oh, Callum," she whispered, her entire body going tense as she exploded into a million pieces, panting as the most wonderous feeling washed over her body.

Ruby plopped back onto the bed but before she could even recover, she felt his mouth on that same spot and looked down, eyes wide as his tongue flicked out and yet a new round of pleasure began. "Oh, my… oh…" words escaped her, as did small breaths as Callum did something so erotic with his tongue that she couldn't stop staring in awe. By god, she had no idea such a thing even existed but it was the single most intensely pleasurable sensation she had ever felt. Another wave flooded her and this time she did scream out as her entire body tensed.

It was as if little explosions were going off behind her eyes and she gripped the sheets, writhing as Callum slowed down but didn't quite stop until she was splayed out on the bed, feeling weak and dizzy, wondering what had just happened to her.

"What was that?" she gasped, looking at him, and he grinned.

"Pleasure, lass. And, ye are still a maiden, as I promised yer father ye would remain." Crawling back up her body, Callum swept sweaty tendrils of hair away from her face, then kissed her so gently on the lips that she thought her heart might actually burst. These feelings were dangerous. She had no remorse for what had just happened. If she was to be united with a man she did not love for the rest of her life, at least she had this memory to cherish.

Still, she would never see Callum again after tomorrow and that thought made her stomach twist up into knots. If this was her last day with Callum, she did not want this moment to end, and even if she, one day, was no more than a whisper in his memory, for her this would be her greatest day and she wished to know more about him.

"Who are you, Callum?"

His head snapped up and his brow rose. "Ye ken who I am. Lord Argyll. Callum Campbell. Scottish pirate. And..." Cupping her face between both of his large hands, he gave her a soft kiss before continuing. "I am a man in love for the first time in his life." Leaning in, he kissed her slowly, deeply, lingering for several moments with his hands still on her cheeks and hers on his waist as she tried to steady herself. A man in love? With her?

When he pulled back and looked at her, she saw the worry in his eyes and frowned. "I do not understand."

"Nor do I," he sighed. "Why now, of all times? Why ye, of all lassies? A lass on her way to wed another man." Callum took her hands and held them. "I love ye, Ruby Berry. I kenned the moment I saw ye, I was a lost man."

"I… I…" Ruby could not answer him. What could she say? That she was madly in love with him, as well, and that she would live in misery the rest of her days, knowing the man who owned her heart sailed the ocean, living the life she longed for, while she sat in a manor home alone, raising children for a man she never saw and never wished to see? "Callum, I… we cannot…" Shaking her head, she felt a tear slip down her cheek and he wiped it away.

"Cannae we?" he asked, sitting up and gripping her shoulders, pulling her onto his lap as he had the first night they kissed. Only this time they were both completely naked and his hardness rested on her thigh.

"No, we cannot. I am betrothed, Callum. My father would kill us both. And I enjoy being on a ship, but I cannot live upon one. I must have a home."

Callum snorted and shook his head. "Ye think me a landless lord?"

Shrugging, Ruby frowned. "I know nothing of you, Callum. I am not even sure what you are asking of me."

"Ruby, I am the Earl of Argyll. I live in my family's ancestral home, Inveraray Castle. I manage the lands and have many duties. In fact, I am on my way back there once I deliver ye to London. I am also a pirate, as ye ken. As for my father, he was killed by—" Callum abruptly stopped and gave her a strange look, before continuing. "I took over the title but was a pirate long before. I manage both quite well, ye ken." He smiled and she shook her head.

"I had no idea. I am terribly sorry about your father, Callum." Ruby sat on the edge of the bed and he followed, sitting beside her and taking her hand.

"Thank ye, love. He was a good man. I have learned to live life on my own terms. One never knows when death is coming. When it does, I wish to ken I lived a good life. Ruby, I enjoy my life. Every day is a new adventure on the seas. When I am home, I manage my tenants, host lavish parties, and do my duties for my government. But when I am on the sea, I am free."

She sighed, wishing she could live such a life… a life with him. But she simply could not. Still, she had now. This moment. Wrapped up in his arms, feeling his heartbeat beneath her palm resting on his chest, his skin warming hers as he surrounded her with his embrace. "Callum, make love to me." Placing her hand on his rock hard, pulsing length, she took it in her hand as she sat on top of him again. Her breasts rested against his chest and Ruby stared into his green eyes, the color of the moss that covered the rocks in the lake near her home. She would always think of him whenever she visited that place for the rest of her life. "I won't see you ever again after tomorrow, but I know I will never regret this. Please, Callum."

His eyes closed and a strained look contorted his features. "Ye torture me, love. I cannae." He shook his head and began to move her off his lap, but she placed her hands on his shoulders and stood her ground.

"You promised to allow me to make my own decisions."

"Aye, I did! But ye ask too much of me, woman! I cannae make love to ye, take yer maidenhead, and then allow ye to walk into the arms of another man! Devil's bollocks, I am delivering ye to yer wedding. Ye torture me, Ruby!" he shouted, trying to push her off.

"Callum! I love you, too!" she blurted, and he froze, slowly opening his eyes and taking a deep breath.

"Ye do?"

"Of course I do, you stubborn Scot. Make love to me."

"Only on one condition. I have another proposal fer ye," Callum said, running his hands up and down her waist, caressing her breasts and making gooseflesh break out all over her body.

"Oh? And what is it you propose this time, Lord Argyll?" she whispered, closing her eyes and enjoying the feel of his hands roaming her body.

"I propose ye marry me, lass. Ruby Berry, I have only kenned ye for three days, and yet I ken without a doubt ye are the only woman I could ever love, will ever love. Will ye be my wife?"

"Capt'n! A ship can be seen on the horizon!" The loud bang of Samuel's fist on the door made Ruby jump and squeal, clinging to Callum before she could even answer his question, let alone consider all that he had just said.

Cursing in a language Ruby could not understand, Callum jumped up and pulled his breeches on, tossing her clothing to her at the same time. "Get dressed, love." Once she was very hastily clothed and he had pulled the tunic over his head and strapped on his sword, Callum opened the door with a grumble of frustration, Ruby standing behind his shoulder. "And? What flag do they fly?"

"Ye willnae like the answer…" Samuel looked over Callum's shoulder and frowned in Ruby's direction, making her feel a sense of dread. Why was he looking at her that way?

"Well? Spit it out, Samuel!" Callum demanded, grabbing the spyglass from his first mate's hand and storming on to the deck, looking out to sea. Ruby followed him, anxious to know who approached and why Samuel appeared so frazzled.

"Devil's bollocks!" Callum slammed his fist down on the rail and Ruby touched his elbow.

"Who is it?" she whispered, half afraid to know.

Lowering the glass, Callum looked down at her and crinkled his brow. "'Tis yer betrothed. And he has yer father."

Chapter 7

"Ready the cannons! We will pursue the bastard! Prepare for a fight, lads!"

His crew all ran to do their duties, knowing exactly what he expected and doing it well while he stood at the helm with Ruby by his side.

"I hardly think all that is necessary, Callum. 'Tis just my father and William. Though, I do not wish to go back with him." The dread in her quivering voice and the blanching of her face were all Callum needed to see, to know she feared what was to come, and she did not even know the worst of it yet. "I wish to stay with you, Callum. I will tell my father. Come what may, I am not leaving you."

Clenching his fist and looking through the spyglass once more, he could clearly make out the details now that he had hoped were no more than a trick of the light previously.

"Ruby." Callum grabbed her hand and pulled her to him. "I need ye to listen to me well. William is a pirate hunter. He is the man responsible for my father's death. He has yer father tied up on his deck."

"What?" Ruby gasped and ripped the glass from his hand, her hands quivering so much he wondered if she could see properly. "No… no!" Lowering the glass, she looked at Callum and glowered. "Why didn't you tell me? Tell my father? He deserved to know!"

"I tried, lass. I warned yer father before we left, if ye recall, after William threatened him. It was not a false threat. I meant to tell ye, Ruby. I was going to tell ye before I let ye go to him. I simply believed I had more time. It isnae an easy thing to tell a woman that her future husband is a murderer. I am sorry."

Ruby pursed her lips and squeezed her eyes shut. "My papa. Why would William do this? How does he even have my father? He left before us!"

"Yer father put too much trust in the man. He was safe until he was caught doing business with me. I am a Scottish heathen, after all. Now William kens yer father must have Stuart sympathies, and that is dangerous information. Likely, he went back for him and expected to marry ye before ye kenned he had yer father in custody. He will flee from us when we give chase because he meant to reach London and handle yer father before ye arrived. He never wished for ye to see his evil deeds, love. We will get him, Ruby. I vow it."

Raising her chin higher, Ruby looked at the ship approaching them, the British flag whipping in the wind, and narrowed her eyes in determination. "Yes. We will."

Callum smiled, seeing that spark in her eyes and the fire in her blood that had made him immediately fall in love with her in the first place.

"He will use yer father to control ye, love. He will demand ye board his ship, but dinnae do it. Allow me to control the situation."

"What if he harms him when I do not obey? I cannot allow that! I must do something more than simply stand by!" she demanded with panic in her small voice.

"We dinnae have time to make a plan. Follow my lead and follow yer instincts. Trust them. I do. We can do this together."

"Together." Ruby gave him back the glass and balled her fists into the fabric of her skirt until her knuckles turned white. She looked beautiful and full of determination as the blue and white Scottish flag whipped wildly above them. He had his ship, his men, his woman, and his country. What pirate needed more? They would save her father and he would marry Ruby. But first, he was going to slay the man who betrayed his father.

"What do ye wish to do, Capt'n?" Samuel came up behind them and eyed them oddly as if he knew what had transpired between them in the cabin, but Callum did not care. He was not ashamed of his actions, nor his feelings for Ruby, and he had bigger issues to deal with at the moment.

"I wish to kill that bastard once and fer all. But first, we will rescue Thomas Berry and kill every man aboard that ship if we must. Take no quarter, if necessary. Whatever is aboard that ship is ours for the taking."

"Aye, Capt'n." Samuel took off to help ready the ship and Callum turned his attention back to Ruby. William's ship grew closer, yet as Callum suspected, the man was doing his best to evade them, coward that he was. He wished to have her father hung before Ruby married him. She would not know her father was dead until she was stuck with his murderer. A chill ran up Callum's spine. The man was pure evil, but today was his last day on this earth.

"Are ye ready, Ruby?" He was worried for her, despite her strength. Her father was in real danger and he would do all he could to keep them both safe, but William was a madman who kept his deeds hidden in the shadows, away from polite society. But Callum was not polite and he was aware of the evil that lurked in William's eyes.

"Yes, I am."

A warning shot fired as his ship approached and Ruby squealed and jumped, gripping Callum's arm as the cannon missed them by a fair distance, but caused waves that shook the ship violently, nearly knocking her off her feet. Grabbing Ruby to keep her steady, Callum readied himself for the moment he had been waiting for for years. Yet never had he imagined he would be in love with a woman and need to save her father from the bastard before he could gut him.

Callum remained calm and guided his ship closer to William's galleon, ordering his men to throw a grappling hook over the railings to pull the ships closer.

"Stay back until I call for ye, Ruby. Trust me." Callum and Samuel walked over to the rails at the stern where he could clearly see William with Thomas tied up to a mast beside him. The look of fear on the bastard's face was amusing, yet Callum knew the only thing William feared was being found out by Ruby.

"I see ye are bonding with yer future father by marriage," Callum shouted to William who stood on the other side of his railings as his men readied the wooden plank to create a walkway between the ships. Even from this distance, Callum could make out the reddening of William's face and the veins bulging from his neck.

"Where is she?" William growled.

"Of whom do ye speak? The whore who gave ye that bloody lip? It looks horrible, mate."

"You know who, you bastard! This is not how it was meant to be! All was well until you showed up at their home. I knew then he was a Stuart loyalist. I have no choice, Callum! It is my duty to the queen! Send Ruby over now or Thomas dies!"

"No!" Callum heard Ruby shout from behind as she ran to the stern. "Papa! I'm so sorry, Papa!"

"This is not your doing, my dear. You were not meant to be involved in this," William said soothingly, and Callum flared his nostrils in anger and disbelief. The man still spoke sweetly to her, as if she would simply understand and forgive him for what he was doing to her father. "This is his doing and his alone, Ruby. Now, come to me and all will be well."

He was lying and Callum knew it. He would still eventually make certain Thomas hung by a noose and he would attack his ship as soon as Ruby was secured. Looking over at Ruby, he saw the frown on her face and the shaking of her hands, and he knew she understood the truth. "It will be well, Ruby. I vow it. Trust me," Callum whispered so only she could hear.

"Allow me to escort the lady to ye," Callum shouted, but William shook his head.

"Do you think me a fool? I will not allow you, a Scottish pirate, to taint my ship with your presence."

"Then ye will come to me and collect her yerself. She will not go alone."

"Why should I? I have the upper hand, Scotsman! If she does not come, Thomas dies!"

Ruby took a step forward, but Callum put out a hand and held her back, giving her a stern look of warning. He needed her to trust him to handle this. He would have to show no weakness, to pretend not to care what happened to Ruby or her father, and he prayed she would see through his act. It was his only chance to get William to board his ship. "I care not if ye kill the Englishman. He is no friend of mine, and I willnae see Ruby again after today. My cannons are loaded and my men are itching for a fight. They would love to take yer ship, yer goods, and yer lives."

His men roared and raised their swords, cutlasses, knives, and pistols in the air for William and his soft men to see. They were overweight and spoiled, having no idea what it meant to truly fight. Threats were what they thrived on, and Callum knew how to shake the British down. They feared the wild Scots, believed them to be uncivilized, brainless animals from the north who slaughtered Englishmen just to pass the time. Their opinions had never bothered Callum before and now, more than ever, he hoped their unfounded fears benefited his cause.

Ruby pinched the back of his arm in anger at his words, but Callum kept his eyes locked on William. "What say ye? Come get Ruby, alone, or ye all die."

"I can blow your ship to pieces, you Scottish bastard!" William roared.

"I ken ye can. But, ye willnae, not with Ruby onboard. So, come get yer bride or she can die with the rest of ye." Callum shrugged and popped his knuckles, feeling pain inside for having to use Ruby as bait but knowing he had little choice if he was going to get William alone to slay the man and save Thomas.

William went silent for a moment while he thought about his options and finally nodded, apparently deciding he had to obey if he didn't wish for Ruby to die. At least the man had one redeeming quality. He truly did care for Ruby. Unfortunately, Callum would die before he allowed her to spend a lifetime with this man. Even if she did not choose him at the end of this ordeal, he would give her the freedom to live a life of her choosing.

William began walking across the plank with his hand resting on the hilt of his sword and Callum eyed the man warily, ready to draw his weapon if William made one wrong move. The man verily strutted across the plank in his tight breeches and matching surcoat and tunic, all a pristine shade of black with shiny leather boots up to his knees, but Callum saw the quiver of William's hand and knew he was unsure of his position in this confrontation.

Daring a glance at Ruby, Callum saw she was flushed and worried, wringing her hands together and staring across the way at her bound father. "Ye ken I willnae ever allow ye to be harmed, aye?" he whispered in her ear, and her gaze snapped to him. When a small smile crept over her face and she nodded, his heart lifted. She had commented once before that it felt as if they had known each other for years and he could not disagree. Never would he have believed such an intense, consuming connection could be possible, but with Ruby, it was as if they were two halves of one whole and from the moment he saw her, it was impossible to stay away.

Once William stepped onto Callum's deck, Ruby stormed over to William and struck him across the face, making him grunt in pain. No wonder Callum loved this woman. She was fierce and fearless. Still, he needed her to attempt to control her anger. Walking over to her, Callum pulled her away but could not resist flashing her a proud smile.

"How dare you do this, you… you piece of shite bastard!" Ruby spat while Callum held her back.

"You bitch! You have split my lip open again!" William rubbed blood from his lip and lunged to grab Ruby by the arm, but Callum pushed her back toward Samuel and withdrew his sword.

"Insult the lass again and I will kill ye before yer next breath."

"What is this?" William looked between Callum and Ruby, glowering. "I see you have a fondness for the lady, and I cannot blame you. But she is mine. Hand her over," William said with a stuffy, entitled tone that made Callum snort with indignation.

"Ruby belongs to nobody. She is not property. But if ye want her to come with ye, ye will fight me."

"Are ye mad? I will not fight for something that is already mine, and she *is* mine," William scoffed.

"I am not yours and never will be!" Ruby shouted. "You betrayed me and my family!"

William turned toward Ruby and scowled menacingly, the devil beneath his handsome exterior exposed. "He betrayed his queen and country. That is a crime punishable by death." His cool, hard tone bore no emotion, and Ruby kicked out her leg and caught him in the shin before Samuel pulled her back once more, but not before William struck out, catching her across the cheek with the back of his hand. When Ruby grunted in pain and held her face, something in Callum snapped.

Rage burned in Callum's gut and he yearned for the justice and revenge he had plotted for years. "That was yer final mistake, Vice-Admiral. Ye are a coward and naught more. Ye stabbed my father in the back, betrayed Ruby's father, and ye hit the woman I love. Now, ye will die."

Callum gripped his sword's hilt tighter and got into a fighting stance, staring his father's killer down, ready to rid the world of this scum. He could feel the blood pumping through his veins as his heart beat wildly, thirsting to spill the blood of his enemy, the ancient blood lust of warriors and men facing their foe.

"The woman you love?" William growled and looked at Ruby. "Is this true? Do you love him, as well?"

Ruby narrowed her eyes and stepped closer to Callum, but Samuel held her back, keeping her away from the inevitable violence. "Yes. I do love him, William. I shall not marry you. I never wished to, and I will die before I marry you for what you have done to my father and his!"

Taking a deep, eerie breath, William's eyes widened and his nostrils flared with contempt and hurt pride. "Have you played his whore then, you wanton bitch? I will kill you both, then watch with glee as your father dangles by a rope!" William's hand twitched at his side and Callum drew his sword, preparing to run William through the moment the man went to strike. Instead, he saw a long wooden object swiftly being pulled out of William's ruffled tunic sleeve, so quickly that Callum had no time to think before he heard a pistol being cocked and saw it pointed straight at Ruby's heart.

"Nay!" Everything around him moved in slow motion, every detail of that second feeling like an eternity. The blast of the pistol, the spark and the smoke, the bullet ripping through his flesh, the searing agony in his chest. A second shot rang out immediately, just as Callum felt his body colliding with the deck of his ship with a painful thud, his head hitting the wooden planks with a force strong enough to split his skull.

Shouts surrounded him. Another body fell with an audible thud and grunt beside him and Ruby screamed when full battle between the ships' crews burst out. "R—" Callum tried to say her name but the pain lashing through his chest and the metallic taste of blood surging up his throat choked him, his words disappearing along with his consciousness while the ringing in his ears dimmed with the fading sounds of cannon fire. A black haze washed him away into oblivion darker and colder than the deepest waters he had ever sailed, and though he tried to reach out to find his Ruby, to pray she was not the other person who had fallen, Callum felt as if boulders pinned his limbs down, even as he heard his name whispered in her voice one last time.

Chapter 8

Rocking in the ornately carved oak chair near the hearth, Ruby sighed and stared at the leaping flames for the fifth night in a row since arriving at Inveraray Castle in Scotland while the doctor checked Callum's stitches for signs of infection, though they seemed to be healing well. It had been eleven days since the battle that changed her life forever.

Closing her eyes, the sounds of cannon fire and the smell of gunpowder provoked terrorizing memories, but none worse than the sight of Callum falling to the deck after taking a bullet meant for her, followed by the body of William. Both men fell within seconds of one another from bullet wounds.

Fortunately for Callum, the bullet had missed any major organs and had miraculously gone through one side and out the other, tearing through tissue but hitting no bones. William had not been so fortunate. Ruby had aimed directly for his head and she never missed her mark. She had been damned certain of her shooting abilities when smuggling the pistol into her boot before leaving Callum's cabin that afternoon. Her decision had ended one life, but it had saved many more. She would shoot that pistol again in a heartbeat if necessary, but the reality of having taken a man's life sat heavily on her soul.

A knock on the chamber door made her ruminations of the past disappear like the tendrils of smoke in the hearth, floating up the chimney and out into the early autumn breeze. Standing from the chair, Ruby cleared her throat and walked over to the door to allow Callum's most frequent visitor to enter, then walked over to the bed where Callum lay once more with his eyes closed, and she flinched against another stab of pain to her heart. Why, damn it all? Why had he taken that bullet? It had been meant for her and she would have gladly taken it. The man she loved, who had had so much fire and life inside him, had slept for eleven days, thrashing at times from pain and the fever burning his flesh, but otherwise silent and distant, suffering in a faraway place where Ruby could not reach him despite her many attempts. "He appears better today, yes?"

Ruby looked at her father and nodded, squeezing his hand as she gave him a weak smile. She thanked God every day for the safe return of her father after the battle. Callum's men had fought hard and fought well, prevailing over the English and following Callum's command to take no quarter if necessary, and it had been. The men aboard William's ship proved just as violent and ignorant as their Vice-Admiral, all trying to kill men simply for being born in a land north of their own. Her father had been unbound and taken on board, where he used his own healing skills from years of experience at sea to stitch up Callum's wounds. If not for Callum, her father might have died. If not for her father, Callum might have died. Life was filled with too many variables to consider. The only things that mattered were the two men in this room with her now.

"Aye, Sir Berry. Our Earl is improving daily." The doctor finally spoke once he was finished checking Callum's wound. "I dinnae ken what else to do. His fever has broken and his wound is healing quite nicely. All he needs to do is awaken."

"What can we do to help with that?" her father asked, gripping her hand tightly to give her support.

"Pray, my lord. 'Tis all ye can do for the Earl now. He is home and he is alive and healing. In fact, his unconsciousness is a blessing, for he is almost fully healed, thanks to yer quick work and steady hand aboard the ship. The man has slept through the agony and should awaken with nearly no more pains," he said, snapping his black leather satchel shut and pointing up at the heavens.

"All I have done is pray and yet naught has happened," Ruby said petulantly, wanting nothing more than to see his cursed eyelashes flutter.

"Aye, something has. He is healing. Keep praying, lass." Doctor Ferghus Campbell touched her cheek gently and squinted, leaning in. "Yer bruise is clearing up quite well. Curse the soul of the man who did that to ye."

"Oh, his soul is cursed. Make no mistake," her father replied, looking at her with a frown. It broke her heart to see her papa suffering so. She wanted to reassure him that she was all right, but that would be a lie. Nothing would be all right until Callum awoke once more. Until then, she would stay in this chamber every moment by his side.

As the doctor tipped his hat and walked toward the door, her father shuffled up to her side and stroked her hair. "You really love him."

"I do. Is that odd? To know something so entirely in your bones, to feel it so deeply and after only days of knowing a person? Am I a fool?"

"Heavens no, my sweet girl. It is rare, I will give you that. But you've never been a woman prone to dramatics... well..." he chuckled and looked down at Callum. "At least not until he came along. But you knew, and you followed him. I cannot be mad. You should be mad at me for forcing you to marry that foul, festering boil of a man!"

"Oh, Papa. You did not know. How could you have? All is well now. Or, it will be soon, I pray."

"Well, when Lord Argyll awakens, I will be giving him my blessing to marry my daughter."

A tear ran down Ruby's cheek and she jumped on her father with a squeal. "Oh, thank you, Papa! I do not wish to speak for Callum, but I daresay he will be pleased!"

"Ye neednae... speak for me... love." Callum's raspy, weak voice carried to her ears and she spun around, looking down at him and seeing his beautiful green eyes looking back at her for the first time in eleven days with pure elation flooding her.

"Callum! Oh, you are awake!" She ran to his side and grabbed his hand, gently sitting on the edge of the bed.

"Either I... am awake, or I am... dead and in heaven, which I assure ye is... unlikely," he whispered and licked his cracked lips. Ruby propped him up and set a glass of water to his lips and he successfully swallowed a small amount before she put it back on the table near the bed.

"Welcome back to the land of the living, son." Callum struggled to keep his eyes open but he smiled in her father's direction.

"Thank ye, Sir Thomas."

"Papa! Please run and tell everyone their laird is awake! And bring him some broth!" Utter joy filled Ruby as she sat beside Callum and felt the warmth of his hands in hers. More tears dripped down her cheeks, but she wiped them away and refused to let more fall, lest they blur her vision and prevent her

122

from seeing his chiseled, handsome face, even if he was slightly paler and thinner now. He was alive and well-healed and soon, he would gain his weight back and be as good as new.

Her father nodded and left the room with haste, and Ruby leaned down to kiss Callum's forehead. "I was so worried, love. Why did you take that bullet for me? I am so angry with you."

"I would do it a million times over."

"And I would shoot William a million times over to save you."

"Ye shot William? I thought I had lost ye, Ruby. When I fell, I heard ye scream. I thought ye were shot. I have been stuck in a world where I believed ye were dead, trapped in my mind, mourning yer loss."

"I am well, love. And yes, I shot him with your pistol from your cabin. We won't ever worry about him again."

When a serving lass came through the chamber door holding a large bowl of steaming brown broth, Ruby took it and helped Callum drink it down, urging him to continue until it was gone. He needed nourishment to gain his strength back.

"I dinnae wish to take my eyes off of ye, but I am verra tired." Callum's eyes began to flutter closed once more and Ruby gasped, scared he would fall asleep for another several days once more. "Dinna fash, lass. I will awaken by the morn, I vow. Now that I ken ye are here with me, I have too much to lose. Here." Callum patted the bed beside him. "I wish to lay with ye, if I may."

"Of course!" Ruby wished for privacy for Callum so he could sleep uninterrupted. Closing and barring the door behind her, Ruby removed her dress, leaving her linen shift on, and climbed under the covers, feeling his warmth surround her. Facing him, Ruby smiled and kissed him gently, sweeping a dark lock of hair away from his face.

"Sleep now. I shall be here when you awaken. I love you, Callum," she whispered, closing her eyes.

"I love ye too, my fierce pirate wench." He smiled before his face relaxed and his eyes fluttered shut, his soft breaths fanning her face with a peaceful rhythm.

A wee bit of sun filtered through his eyelids and, after days of nothing but darkness, it was enough to remind him that he was still alive, as was the soft woman still wrapped in his arms.

Cracking one eyelid open, Callum observed Ruby up close and wondered how he, a bloody arse of a Scottish pirate, had gotten so damned fortunate to have this wee exquisite English rose in his bed. And, she loved him. How or why was a mystery to him and always would be. As would be the immediate connection they had formed. His father had always said he loved his mother upon first sight, but Callum had balked at that, believing such ideals to be for fools. Mayhap they were. He was the greatest fool he had ever known for reasons too numerous to count, and yet, he had the love of the most incredible woman.

Up close, he saw a small dusting of freckles dotting her nose. They were so faint that he would never know they existed if not for the honor of holding her so close and watching her while she slept. Her long black lashes swept against the curve of her high cheekbones and he admired the small pout of her pink lips. He would pinch himself if both hands were not better occupied, wrapped around her small waist.

When her eyes began to flutter open, he smiled and felt that familiar tug in his heart that he had only ever felt for this one woman. He had been asleep for so many days, with his mind thinking she was lost to him, torturing him with pain beyond comprehension, he had believed himself dead, and better off so. Now, feeling her warmth, seeing her blue eyes scan his features, he wondered how he had ever lived his life believing he was incapable of loving a woman or wishing for a wife.

"Good morning, my handsome, healthy Scottish heathen," she chimed, stretching in his arms and smiling at him. Her arms rested against his bare chest, just above his wound site, and he was pleased not to feel any more searing pain when he tested it with a slight twist of his torso.

"Good morn to ye, my bonnie brave English lass. How do ye feel?"

"Me? You are asking me how I feel when you were shot through the chest and slept for eleven days. I am in your arms and you are alive. I have never been better. I care more about how you are doing, Callum."

"Well, let me see…" Callum reached under the covers and touched his wound, feeling no pain. Then, he touched her bared leg and grinned. "I feel no pain and I have the leg of a goddess wrapped around me. I believe I am quite well, love. And I still have all my limbs," he said, waggling his brows.

Her face turned red when she felt his cock against her stomach, and she giggled. "You sure do. But you had better control that before you injure yourself again."

"Lass…" Callum flipped over, propping himself up on his elbows as he hovered above her. "There is no amount of pain I would not endure to be close to ye, but I assure ye the only part of me that aches is my back from lying on it so long and well…" he winked at her and she laughed, wrapping her arms around his neck.

"Well, I most certainly am pleased to hear that you are hale. And I certainly wish to do all that I can to alleviate any of your discomforts," she said with a sly grin and slowly lowered her hand between their bodies, placing it on the evidence of his arousal beneath his breeches. He closed his eyes and groaned. After having felt so much pain, not only from the bullet wound but from believing Ruby dead, feeling just the barest touch from her felt like the world's greatest gift. He did not want to press her for anything she did not wish to give, but he wanted to connect with her, be the man who made love to her first and forever.

"Ruby," Callum murmured and closed his eyes, enjoying the feel of her. "I want to make love to ye right now." Running a hand up her bare thigh, he guided his fingers to her core and groaned again when he felt her wet heat.

"I want to Callum, but are you well enough? We have time. Do not injure yourself again."

"I am more than well enough, love. And one thing I have learned is that we never ken just how much time we have. Let me show ye now, here, today, how much I love ye, how much I need ye."

Looking him in the eye, Ruby smiled and nodded. "I need you too, Callum. I want this with you."

"Ye are the most beautiful woman in the world, Ruby Berry." Getting on his knees, Callum pushed his breeches down his hips, then slipped her shift up her body and over her breasts, needing to see more of her. When those perfect luscious mounds were freed and her nipples puckered from the morning chill of the room, Callum bent over to tenderly kiss each one, pleased when she tilted her head back and sighed.

"I love ye and always want to be the man to make ye sigh with pleasure." Callum shifted between her legs and pressed his erection to her entrance, feeling her softness and wishing to bury himself completely. But before he would allow himself to take her maidenhead, he needed to make certain she was truly his. "But, ye never answered my question."

Her eyes opened and the flush of her cheeks warmed his heart. So much innocence, yet she was the greatest seductress he had ever known. "What question?" She wrinkled her brow and chewed her bottom lip, making him want to devour her mouth.

"Ruby Berry, will ye become Ruby Campbell, Countess of Argyll and make Scotland yer home? Will ye marry me? I vow to always give ye adventure upon the high seas when we can break away from our responsibilities here. I vow to always give ye freedom to make yer own decisions… except dancing around my men in breeches. I shall not allow that." He smirked and her tinkling laughter made his heart soar. "Will ye marry me and make me whole for the first time in my life?"

"Yes!" Ruby threw her hands around his neck and kissed him all over his face. "Yes, I shall marry you, Callum Campbell! I never wished for a title, but my mother shall be pleased by it," she chuckled. "We will make our life one grand adventure, both on land and at sea."

"I love ye, Ruby. And I always will." Callum kissed her softly, slowly, lingeringly, allowing his tongue to meld with hers until the ache to be one with her was more than he could bear. She was his future wife now. It felt like a dream to know the woman who stole his breath away only days ago was now going to be his wife. Slowly sheathing himself inside her warmth, Callum groaned, feeling her surround him as her legs wrapped around his hips, and she arched her back with a sigh.

He felt her barrier and knew it would sting. He had never bedded a maiden and wasn't sure if he should be quick or slow. "This is said to hurt a wee bit, love."

"I do not care, just do it," she whispered. "I am ready." Nodding, Callum drove himself into her and she hissed and flinched, but within seconds she relaxed and began to move with him. The pleasure was so intense he had to grit his teeth to prevent losing himself too soon. She was so soft and her sweet floral scent floated around her. The room was cold but their bodies were on fire, moving in tandem as they experienced their first taste of real love together.

Ruby groaned and opened her eyes, looking down to watch as he moved inside her. The woman would be his undoing, he vowed. His pace quickened and his arms shook, the weakness of days of healing starting to take their toll. But nothing was going to ruin this moment for him. He may ache a wee bit more than he let on, but it had been worth it to finally be with her, to feel himself inside her for the first time.

Reaching between their connected bodies, Callum placed his finger on the same spot that had driven her mad once before, and her gasp as she inhaled and the moan of pleasure she released, told him she was close to her climax. "Let it go, love," he murmured, moving with her, feeling his own pleasure ready to explode any second.

Together, their bodies shuddered as waves of unfettered pleasure released and they shook in one another's arms before both going limp. By all that was holy, Ruby would be the death of him, but he would gladly die in her arms if it meant they could share this connection for the rest of their lives.

Panting, Ruby pushed her blonde tendrils away from her face as Callum rolled over and wrapped his arm around her waist, pulling her closer. "That was…"

"Unbelievable," Callum whispered, nibbling on her ear. "Unlike anything I have ever experienced," he added.

"Is that what I have been missing out on?" she giggled and rolled toward him, her breasts close enough to his mouth that he could not resist the need to devour them.

"Nay," he mumbled as he sucked her nipple into his mouth, enjoying how it hardened in response and the way her hips arched into his. "I believe what we experienced is the unique reunion of souls, love." He sounded like a bloody lovesick fool, even to his own ears, but nothing about this connection was usual and he could describe it in no other way. They were soul bound and he may not consider himself a religious man, but he was certain there was a higher power drawing them together.

"I agree. I may not know what it is like to be with another man, but I cannot deny the instant pull toward you, my immediate trust in you. I think I just knew I was meant to be yours."

"Well then," Callum said slowly, flicking his tongue over her breasts before moving up the slim column of her neck. "How long must I wait to officially make ye mine, love? I wish to marry ye as soon as possible."

"I am already yours. But if you can let me out of bed at any time today, I shall speak with my father and make arrangements." Kissing him on the cheek, Ruby hopped out of bed, but he pulled her back down, making her squeal with laughter.

"Verra well. I shall rest a wee bit while ye are gone, but I warn ye, I am not done with ye for the day." He waggled his brows and she smiled, pulling her dress on and tightening the laces.

"I look forward to it," she winked and left the room with a flourish. Callum sighed and stared at the ceiling, wondering how he had become so fortunate a man and such a besotted fool. Grinning like an arse for the dozenth time that morning, Callum carefully climbed out of bed and decided to do some planning of his own. He may be weak, but he needed to be out of this bed. Besides, he had a bride to marry, a wedding to plan, and a future father by marriage to speak with. Ruby would become part of the Campbell clan as soon as possible, and he planned on making it a day she would never forget.

Chapter 9

The seat of the Campbell clan was a massive castle unlike anything Ruby had ever seen, and by the end of the day, she would be the Countess of Argyll and the lady of the castle. Though trepidation flooded her insides, Ruby was ready for the next big adventure.

Callum had refused to lay abed and rest since the day she agreed to marry him. A sennight had passed with him showing Ruby the lands, introducing her to the lovely tenants and staff of the house, as well as meeting his strange yet kind first cousin, Charles Campbell, who was a knight for the Stuarts and very popular with the lassies of the keep. Charles had just returned to the castle to discover his cousin had been wounded, but the two men seemed rather close, and Ruby was pleased Callum had a companion here to care for him when she was busy around the keep.

Callum's mother had passed when he was born and an ache had settled in her belly for him having grown up without a mother. How she wished her mother could have been here to see them get married. She was opinionated and full of pride, but she was a loving woman who would wish to be here. Her father had recovered entirely from his ordeal with William, having only sustained mild bruising in the process, and had been given the ship he had been captured on. Callum had many ships and few men he could trust. Ruby enjoyed watching her father and Callum discuss their travels, making plans for more.

As Ruby was surrounded by some of the young serving lassies who prepared her for her wedding day, they all laughed and gossiped while one of them named Isabella twisted Ruby's curls up and tucked fresh flowers into some of her braids.

"Ye ken, none of us thought our laird would ever get married," one of the lassies who was close to Ruby's age said definitively. "He was here, and then he was gone. He took care of us, he did. But at times, we didnae ken if our laird and earl would ever return."

"Aye, and he almost didnae," another lass added, pulling the laces tight on the bodice of Ruby's flowing blue damask dress with long sleeves that fell below her wrists and a modestly cut neckline. The color matched her eyes and she felt beautiful and truly loved. Unlike her wedding to William, Ruby absolutely could not wait to meet Callum in front of the kirk doors. It felt as if this day could not get any better.

A knock on the door made Ruby's head turn just as Isabella placed the last flower in her hair and stepped away. "Come in, as long as ye arenae the groom! 'Tis bad luck for him to see the bride!" Marla, one of the older women in the chamber shouted.

"No, no. 'Tis only me."

"Papa!" Ruby stood up from her seat and walked over to her father, who wore an approving, proud smile that made Ruby flutter all over. It all felt like a dream. Just over a fortnight ago she had met Callum and now he meant everything to her and even her father was smiling.

"You look wonderful, my darling." Thomas looked her up and down and smiled widely. "I did not mean to interrupt, but I have a little surprise for you."

"You do?" she asked, wondering what he could possibly mean. Her father stepped aside and Ruby covered her mouth with her hands, gasping as tears threatened to spill when she saw who stepped through the door. "Mama?" Running to her mother, Ruby threw her arms around her and cried, a feeling of completeness filling her. "How?"

"Do you think I would miss my daughter's wedding, Ruby? To an earl, no less!"

"Well... I... did not think you would entirely approve."

Penelope waved away her concerns. "I only wish for your happiness. It was wrong of us to choose William on your behalf. I see that now. When your father went missing, a man from the dock said he saw him being taken away by the Vice-Admiral, charged with treason for doing business with a Scottish pirate and for having Stuart sympathies. Did you believe I would not follow? Nobody takes off with my husband, Ruby. I have not survived being the wife of a pirate—"

"Privateer," her father interrupted with a wink, and Penelope laughed and rolled her eyes.

"Call it what you will. I have learned a thing or two in my time. I caught a smaller boat and paid my way to London. When I was informed that William's ship was lost at sea, taken by Callum, I changed my destination and came to Scotland. I knew Callum would not risk harm to you or your father. And here you all are. I owe everything to Lord Argyll. I am very proud of you… lass."

Ruby laughed, wiping away her tears when her mother attempted to speak like a Scot. "You are so brave, Mama. I had no idea…"

"I know you did not. Because I have always tried to protect you from this life, Ruby. It is not for the faint of heart. One day you are in your home sharing a meal with your family, and the next day, your daughter is aboard a pirate ship, and your husband is captured by a snake in the grass. Yet, I see now that you have found your place and your partner in life. You are no longer my little girl."

Words escaped Ruby as she embraced her mother, her throat stinging as she choked back more tears. She did not wish to arrive at her wedding with red, swollen eyes. Never had she felt such a great sense of belonging and excitement for her future.

"My Lady. 'Tis time," one of the maids said, and Ruby's heart skipped a beat. She nodded and took her father's arm in one hand and her mother's in the other as they walked out of the chamber and down the tower stairs, toward the keep. The entire place was empty and Ruby grew nervous, knowing every resident of the castle and all of the tenants would be awaiting her arrival, but she just focused on seeing Callum, who she had not been allowed to see all cursed day thanks to the serving lassies who did all they could to keep him away, despite his best attempts. When she awoke that morning, a single rose and a letter expressing his love had been awaiting her on her bed, and Ruby glowed with adoration for the man she would soon marry.

When they walked out of the hall and into the inner bailey, Ruby attempted to turn left toward the kirk, but her parents insisted they continue straight outside the gates. "The kirk is not that way, Papa. That is the waterfront."

"I know, Ruby," he said with a grin, giving her a wink.

"I do not understand… my wedding is over there…"

"But your groom is over there," her mother said wryly, pointing toward her father's newly acquired ship in the distance.

"He is on Papa's ship? But…" Squinting as they grew closer, she saw the name "Penelope" freshly painted on the side of his ship and smiled, happy that her parents were so in love after all these years and yet confused about what was happening.

The ship appeared to be filled to the brim with people, and the closer Ruby came the more she could make out. Ribbons and fine cloths of gold were draped over the sides of the ship, sparkling in the light of the afternoon sun. "What is happening?"

Nobody seemed to wish to tell her, and when she looked back at the maids following behind, they all just smirked and shrugged, clearly in on whatever was going on.

Even the gangway leading to the ship had gold cloth draped over its rails and when Ruby looked up as she slowly stepped, she saw Callum looking more handsome than ever, awaiting her at the top with a proud grin that made her melt all over and feel so weightless, she thought she might fly away.

"What is happening?" she asked as he took her hand and guided her onto the main deck, where floral arrangements decorated every corner and mast.

"We are getting married," he responded just as her father stepped up in front of them and everyone gathered around.

"Here? On this ship?"

"Aye. On yer father's ship, where he is the captain. Ye ken a captain has the right to marry a couple aboard his ship."

Ruby gasped and clutched her heart, looking at her father, certain more tears would stream down her face. "You are going to marry us, Papa?"

He nodded and puffed out his chest with pride and Ruby could not contain her surprise and elation. Flinging herself against her father, she hugged him fiercely, then did the same to Callum. "It is perfect. Absolutely wonderful. My dream."

Callum chuckled and took her hand. "I assumed as much. I want today to be the very best day of yer life, Ruby. We only get to do this once in a lifetime, and I wish it to be all ye ever wanted."

"Callum, you are all I ever want or need. But this… this is… 'tis perfect. Thank you." She kissed his cheek and they turned to her father, who began the ceremony, reading traditional vows and some she had never heard before, probably from the Scottish traditions. Looking at Callum, she said her vows and felt as if she were floating above herself on a cloud. Could she really be marrying this handsome earl by day, pirate by night, whose dark hair was slicked back into a perfect queue with skintight black breeches, a crisp white tunic, and a matching black surcoat, the Campbell plaid draped and pinned meticulously over his shoulder? He was a sight to behold and she felt herself blushing as she remembered the many nights they had stayed up late making love and exploring one another. He had taught her so many new ways to express herself and she looked forward to a lifetime of learning so much more.

Her father declared them married and named her the new Lady of Inveraray Castle and Countess of Argyll. Before Callum kissed her, Charles walked up, carrying a folded length of the Campbell green and blue plaid, handing it to Callum.

Turning toward Ruby, he smiled down at her and draped the plaid across her shoulders. The blue was the same color as her dress, the green slightly darker than his eyes. "Ye are now Ruby Campbell, a member of our fierce clan. Ye are a Scot now, lass!" Everyone cheered and hollered when he used a heart-shaped pin with a crown atop to secure it, then bent her over without notice, kissing her until she was breathless.

"Ye are my wife now, lass. Any regrets?"

"Many. But none involving you," she said with a giggle and kissed him again.

"Every moment of yer life led ye to the moment when we met, Ruby. Regret nothing. I love ye."

"I love you, Callum Campbell."

Her mother and father hugged her while Charles approached and thumped Callum on the back. "Ye done well, Cousin. She is bonnie, for an English lass," he said with a smirk.

"Maybe if ye stop being an arse, ye will find yerself a bonnie lass to adore and stop looking at my wife, aye?"

Charles rubbed his chin in thought and looked at Ruby once more. "Nay. I cannae make that promise." He smacked Callum on the back once more and hugged Ruby with affection. He was a flirtatious man, but he was harmless and always made her laugh.

Soon everyone departed the ship but stayed close on the harbor as if awaiting something. When Callum made no move to leave the ship, Ruby looked at him and raised a brow. "Well, what now? Are we not going to join our guests for a feast in the hall?"

"We can aye, if ye wish. But I had other plans…"

"Oh?" Ruby pursed her lips, wondering what else Callum could possibly have planned. Letting out a loud whistle, Callum turned her to look at the stairs leading down to the crew's sleeping quarters, and all his men came running up, carrying jugs of ale and the same instruments they had played the day she danced with them.

When they all formed a circle around her and Callum, she laughed and clapped her hands together with excitement. "What is all this?"

"Wife, I took away yer joy on that night. Ye were right. I was jealous and angry because I kenned I loved ye and thought I couldnae have ye. But I should not have been an arse. Tonight, our ship sails away on a new adventure, and ye shall drink all the ale ye wish and dance until yer feet give out, and I shall dance with ye, if I may…" Bending at the waist, Callum put his hand out and she put hers in his, accepting his offer with a laugh as he spun her in a circle and his men began to play.

"Where are we off to, Callum?" she shouted over the music, spinning in her dress with her husband by her side and a crew full of merry pirates, just as she had always wished, yet never dared hope for.

"That is up to ye, lass. The choice, as always, is yers."

When the music stopped, Callum put his hands up to silence his men. "Raise the anchor and ready the sails, lads! I wish to sail the high seas with my wife, the Siren of the Sea!" he shouted and his men whooped, making Ruby laugh with approval at the pirate name he had given her. As the ship began to leave the harbor, Ruby ran over to the railing and leaned over, waving farewell to the Campbell clan who gathered around, shouting their well wishes and waving in return.

"This is all a dream!" she shouted into the wind as her hair blew all around her.

"Nay, love. This is yer life now, our life. And where ye go, I will always follow." Tilting her head back, Callum kissed her with a fierce passion, the way she supposed a pirate should kiss his woman, and she sighed with pure happiness in her heart.

Her life truly was a dream come true.

Author Note

Hello, my lovely reader! I truly hope you enjoyed this swashbuckling romance about Ruby Berry and Callum Campbell! Though this novella was originally written for an anthology, it is not available individually, and I do hope to add more stories to this series!

Though these characters are fictitious creations of my imagination, they are loosely based on real people and events.

In a book called "Uppity Women of Medieval Times" by author Vicki Leon, I read about a fun woman named Lady Killigrew, a noblewoman turned pirate! Her real name was Mary Wolverston and her family were from Suffolk but she married into a powerful ancient Cornish family. Her father was a "gentleman pirate" or a "privateer" but really... he was just a fancy pirate. Piracy ran through her veins and as he wife of a vice-admiral, she became bored of living a kept, fancy life and decided to take matters into her own hands, commandeering a ship of her own and plundering a Spanish ship. She was known to bury treasure in her garden, gentlewoman that she was.

Things for Lady Killigrew did not end well, unfortunately, but I decided to give her new life as Ruby Berry and save her from the stodgy life she was destined to live, instead sending the handsome Callum Campbell to whisk her away to a better fate!

This novella was very fun to write, and I do hope you enjoyed it. I love history and discovering all about forgotten people. If you love stories about strong women throughout time, do pick up a copy of "Uppity Women of Medieval Times" by Vicki Leon and have yourself a ball. I find a lot of inspiration for new characters within those pages! Keep an eye out for more plundering and steamy pirates from me as I work on more books for this series in the future!

Thanks again, Matey, for choosing to read my books and supporting my work! It always means the world to me!

Cheers,

Mia

About the Author

MIA IS THE MOTHER OF two human boys, three dogs, a cat, two guinea pigs, four frogs, and about one dozen fish, residing in the SF Bay Area. How she manages to get anything done is a wonder to all, including herself.

As a child, she often wrote stories about fantastic places or magical things, always preferring to live in a world where the line between reality and fantasy didn't exist. In High school she entered writing contests and had some stories published in small newspapers or school magazines. As life continued, so did her love for writing, along with her passion for history and genealogy, which fuels her creative mind.

When Mia isn't writing books or hanging with her family, she also subs at the local schools, drinks coffee by the gallon, gets lost in a good book, hikes with her family, collects all things pug, and drinks really big margaritas with her friends! Her happy place is the Renaissance Faire, where ye can find her at the joust, rooting for the shirtless highlander in a kilt.

Connect with Mia!

https://linktr.ee/miapride

Also by Mia Pride

Sisters of Danu Series

Forsworn Fate

Forbidden Fate

Foretold Fate

Forgotten Fate

Warriors of Ériu Series

The Warrior's Salvation

The Warrior's Wager

The Warrior's Mission

The Warrior's Reunion

Baby on Board Series

Raising Grace

Tempting Forever

Pirates of Britannica Series

Plunder by Knight

Beast of the Bay

De Wolfe Pack Series

The Lone Wolfe's Lass

The Last Wolfe Lass

Irvines of Drum Series

For Love of a Laird

Like a Laird to a Flame

Maid for the Knight

How to Save a Knight

Pict by Time Series

Where the Thistle Grows

Where the Stars Lead

Where the Ocean Ends

Where the Wolf Howls

Once Upon a Haunted Hillfort

Standalone

Jilted and Kilted

Watch for more at: **www.miapride.com**

www.ingramcontent.com/pod-product-compliance
Lightning Source LLC
Chambersburg PA
CBHW070936130626
46555CB00001B/463